DOUBLE-GUESSED

Horne glanced towards the frigate and saw her bow cutting the waves, changing tack to parallel the *Unity* yet again. He looked over his shoulder; the pattimar had also tacked and was moving directly towards the *Unity*'s stern.

Captain Goodair had also spotted the pattimar's raked sail filled with wind and called, "Prepare larboard guns!"

As the gunner's men laboured the cannons into position, Horne began to suspect the pirates' intentions: the frigate had been used to bait the *Unity*, to lead her into the tack. When Goodair had responded and tacked, the pattimar moved in for what was to appear as a surprise attack from another angle. But during the fleeting minutes in which the *Unity* was preparing to divert aggression from the pattimar, the frigate would give the true death blow.

As the grim realisation dawned that the frigate was double-guessing them, Horne turned to see how far she was abeam. At the same moment, a blast filled the air, timbers crashed onto the deck and he was thrown off his feet . . .

Look for
THE BOMBAY MARINES
and
CHINA FLYER
also by Porter Hill

THE WAR CHEST

An Adam Horne Adventure

Porter Hill

BERKLEY BOOKS, NEW YORK

This is a work of fiction. Names, characters, places, and incidents are either the product of the author's imagination or are used fictitiously, and any resemblance to actual persons, living or dead, business establishments, events, or locales is entirely coincidental.

THE WAR CHEST

A Berkley Book / published by arrangement with
Walker Publishing Company, Inc.

PRINTING HISTORY
Berkley edition / January 2001

The Penguin Putnam Inc. World Wide Web site address is
http://www.penguinputnam.com

ISBN: 0-425-17816-1

BERKLEY®
Berkley Books are published by The Berkley Publishing Group,
a division of Penguin Putnam Inc.,
375 Hudson Street, New York, New York 10014.
BERKLEY and the "B" design
are trademarks belonging to Penguin Putnam Inc.

PRINTED IN THE UNITED STATES OF AMERICA

10 9 8 7 6 5 4 3 2 1

HISTORICAL NOTE

The surrender to the British in 1761 of France's Commander-in-Chief in India, Thomas Lally, prepared the way for the end of the "Seven Years War," but two more years of colonial battles and political intrigue were to pass before England and France reconciled their differences in the Treaty of Paris. This story occurs during the days of uncertain peace in 1761.

Porter Hill

CONTENTS

THE EAST INDIA COMPANY

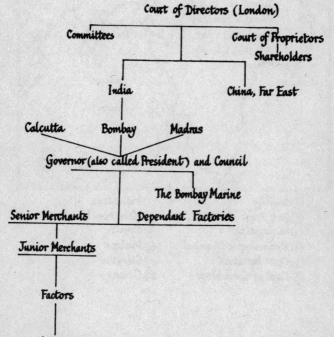

Court of Directors (London)

Committees

Court of Proprietors
Shareholders

India

China, Far East

Calcutta · Bombay · Madras

Governor (also called President) and Council

The Bombay Marine

Senior Merchants

Dependant Factories

Junior Merchants

Factors

Writers

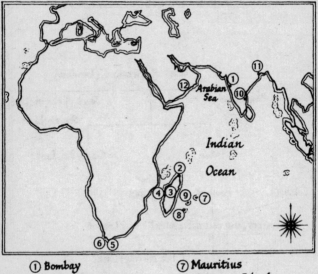

1. Bombay
2. Port Diego-Suarez
3. Madagascar
4. Mozambique Channel
5. Cape Agulhas
6. Cape of Good Hope
7. Mauritius
8. Mascarene Islands
9. Oporto
10. Madras
11. Calcutta
12. Oman

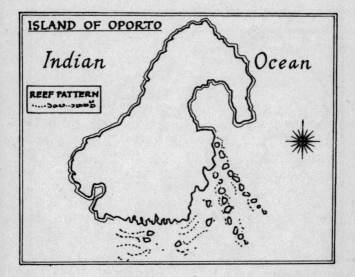

PART ONE
Indiaman

1

Old Voices

Captain Adam Horne stood in a hallway within Bombay Castle, looking down through a narrow window at the jumble of pagodas, clay hovels and tented bazaars crowding the base of the stone fortress. Not daring to speculate on the reason why his Commander-in-Chief, Commodore Watson, had summoned him to headquarters this morning, he clasped his hands behind his blue frock coat and surveyed the activity below him, thinking instead about a letter he had received from his father in London. His eyes following a turbaned man pulling a cart of earthen jars towards a tent, he remembered how angry his father had been when he had first told him that he was joining the Bombay Marine.

Like many fathers whose sons unexpectedly announce that they are going to sea, Horne Senior had argued vehemently against the idea of his only son and heir pursuing a naval career, but finally accepting that Adam would not become a banker like himself, Horne's father had advised him to join the Honourable East India Company's Maritime Service and sail aboard one of the trading company's merchant ships. His alternative suggestion had been to seek a patron in His Majesty's Royal Navy.

Watching as the turbaned man began to unload the pots from his cart, Horne remembered how he had acted against his father's advice and enlisted in the Bombay Marine, the Honourable East India Company's private fighting unit whose job was to safeguard the Company's trading routes.

He closed his eyes in the warm morning sun as he relived those early days. He had felt immediately at home with the small band of troubleshooters when he had joined them eight years ago; contentment had swelled to pride when he had been assigned command of the frigate, the *Eclipse,* thirty-four guns.

More recent memories, though, were not quite so pleasant. Six months ago, the *Eclipse* had been destroyed by the French off the Coromandel Coast, but a worse blow for Horne had been the loss of his crew, leaving him with only seven Marines in his command.

Framed by the castle window, Horne listened to the cacophony of morning noises drift up from the marketplace: the jangle of bells, the cries of fish vendors, the shriek of an elephant and brays of donkeys; his nose caught the intermingling aromas of raw spices, rotting fruits, fish decaying in the sun. The smells of India—accompanied by the ever-present din—reminded him how far away he was from London, both in miles and way of life.

To the right of the stone bastion beneath the window where Horne stood, he could see a crowd gathering around a storyteller sitting on a red carpet, and as he watched the crowd grow, he wondered if he could write to his father, explaining that he was content as a Bombay Marine, that he had been happy during the past eight years in India and had no plans for returning home; he knew he must not postpone that letter any longer, and he must compose more than a few pages. He considered whether he should include details about the last assignment, mention the men he had recruited from prison to form the special squadron he had led into Fort St. George in Madras.

No. Mentioning the mission would be inadvisable. The manoeuvre into Fort St. George had been confidential; the Company's Governors had forbidden Horne to talk about it to anyone, not even to submit a written report about his successful kidnapping of the French Commander-in-Chief, Thomas Lally.

Horne lowered his eyes to a line of tents directly beneath the castle window, where a woman with a jug tied to her back was selling water to passersby. He wondered if he should describe to his father how he had been spending the last six months in Bombay; how he had been landlocked in the city since the mission to Madras, how the rainy season had increased the anxiety of waiting for Commodore Watson to give him a new assignment.

Again, he decided, no. The mention of an uncertain future might sound like an admission of defeat. His father could misconstrue it as a confession that joining the Bombay Marine had been the wrong choice.

Should he try to tell his father how he was looking? Ageing? Sustaining the heat? Escaping the flux and yellow fever and the innumerable other diseases rampant in the Orient?

Wondering how he would appear in his father's eyes, Horne turned from the window and glanced at the gilt-framed mirror hanging at the far end of the hallway. He remembered looking into the same mirror while waiting for his last interview with Commodore Watson, the meeting in which Watson had granted him permission to train prisoners for a special squadron to take into Fort St. George.

The heels of Horne's black boots rang firmly against the stone floor as he moved towards the end of the hallway. Approaching the mirror, he saw the reflection of his goldfaced frock-coat with its high-standing collar and gold epaulettes, the tied breeches, white silk shirt and long, winding stock, all details copied from the formal dress uniform of His Majesty's Royal Navy in an attempt by the East India Company to spruce up its officers of the Bombay Marine.

Raising his eyes, he saw a lock of chestnut hair straying from beneath the front of his cocked hat. He used to worry about sea air and humidity curling his hair, making him look younger than his twenty-eight years. Aboard the *Eclipse,* however, he had learned that older, more seasoned men obeyed him despite his youthful appearance.

Standing a little over six feet, Horne was too tall to see his full reflection in the mirror. As he stooped to get a look at the top of his cocked hat, he heard a door open behind him and, turning, he saw Watson's secretary, Lieutenant Todwell, step out into the hallway.

"Commodore Watson will see you now, Captain Horne."

Horne straightened himself. His heartbeat quickened as he finally allowed himself to speculate about the reason for this morning's interview. After a six months' wait, was Commodore Watson finally assigning him to a new mission?

Moving towards the open door, he said, "Thank you, Lieutenant," and as he passed Todwell, his mind fleetingly returned to the duty of writing home.

If Watson was indeed posting him on a mission, could he write about it to his father, giving him a scrap of consolation that a Marine's life was not indolent and without event? Or was it going to be another closely guarded conspiracy?

Commodore Watson, a big man with bushy eyebrows and fat, drooping jowls, paced his sparsely furnished office. "You've been a good man these past months, Horne," he rasped. "You've not slept on my doorstep like a hound."

"Thank you, sir." Horne sat on a straight-back chair in front of Watson's desk, the cocked hat resting on his left knee, the gold and silver scabbard of his sabre slanting to the floor.

Watson's deep, throaty voice went on, "Losing the *Eclipse* was a blow, Horne. Especially after you brought Lally out of Fort St. George."

Horne remembered how that day's victory had been darkened by a tragedy that still, even now, affected his spirits.

"You've been without a command since then. Six months seems a long time when you're young. I remember myself how difficult it was living on half-pay . . ."

Many commanders might criticise Watson's easy manner with his officers. Horne knew, too, that men of rank might find Watson's administration too relaxed, even slipshod. Like Watson, Horne disagreed with stiff conduct, but he wished that the walrus-like Commodore was not so talkative, that he would not waste time commiserating with him.

Watson paused by his desk. "Charles the Second started paying a retaining fee to unemployed officers," he digressed. "Almost a hundred years ago, it was." He resumed his pacing of the stone floor, dabbing a handkerchief at the folds of his neck. "Half-pay saves a man from starvation, yes. But it's still a damned shame to pull someone off a ship and make him sit around getting boils on his backside, drinking beer with men he doesn't like."

Horne forced himself to remain silent, restraining the impulse to move impatiently on his chair.

Watson raised his watery blue eyes to the rattan sweeps of the punkah fan moving slowly above his desk. "You've been eating well, Horne?" he asked.

The question—its avuncular tone—surprised Horne.

"Why . . . yes. Thank you, sir."

"More than a mountain of rice soaked in Indian hot sauces?"

"I've developed a taste for native dishes, sir," Horne confessed. "A man on my last voyage was an exceedingly good cook. He started me eating Indian food."

"Good cook?" Watson's bushy eyebrows shot up his forehead. "One of those Indian chappies from the prison was a cook?"

"Yes, sir. A very good cook, sir."

"Which one was that?"

"Jingee, sir."

"Ah, Jingee! The one no taller than—" Watson levelled out his right hand from his protuberant stomach, "—yea!"

"Yes, sir. Jingee the Tamil, sir."

Watson went back to pacing his chamber, mopping his bald pate. "You put a lot of time and energy into training those prisoners, Horne. It's a pity not to be using their talents—knives . . . garrottes . . . that Japanese hand-fighting . . ."

"*Karate*, sir."

"*Karate!* Ah, yes! That's the name. *Karate!* And what's the name of that Greek fighting? The one you do, Horne?"

"*Pankration*, sir," answered Horne, adding quickly, "but there's a difference between *Pankration* and *Karate*, sir. For one thing, the Greek form is older. It's said that Greeks travelled to Japan and taught the art of open-hand fighting to the Japanese in exchange for the secret of silk-making."

Watson, standing by the window, was no longer listening to Horne. Gazing down at the harbour spreading beyond the stone wharf, he asked, "Horne, you still see those seven men?"

"Yes, sir. Of course, sir."

"None have signed up with a ship?"

"No, sir. Not yet, sir." The men had been free to join other Company ships, but Horne was pleased they had not. Deciding it would do no harm to guide Watson to the subject of a new mission, he added, "With all due respect, sir, my men have been dodging the press gangs, waiting like myself to hear some word from you about a possible assignment. For a reunion of . . . my squadron, sir."

Watson pointed to the west of Bombay Castle. "A Navy brig's in port this morning. I can smell a press gang a hundred miles away. And there's one right outside my window."

Horne had noticed the Navy brig on his way to Bombay Castle. He had guessed, too, that the weathered ship might be a press gang, thugs from the Royal Navy looking for men to put into service aboard the King's fleet. Admiral

Pocock's ships of the line waited across India in the Bay of Bengal.

"Horne, how soon can you produce your men?"

The suddenness of the question jolted Horne. "Excuse me, sir?"

"Your men? How soon can you muster them to embark on a new mission?"

Horne sat on the edge of the chair. "Immediately, sir."

"By tomorrow morning?"

"By this evening, sir."

Watson turned from the window, his eyes trained on the floor. "Horne, I wish I could give you a few details about your new assignment but—damn it, Horne— they've muzzled me again!"

" 'Muzzled,' sir?"

Watson waved his hand, gesturing that it didn't matter, that Horne should forget what he had just said. "I can only tell you," he said, "that you and your men will sail from Bombay aboard the *Unity*."

In his idle days around Bombay, Horne had spent much of his time sitting in the harbour. He remembered the name of every ship he had seen and said now with surprise, "Sir, the *Unity*'s a Company Indiaman."

"Aye. That's right, Horne. The *Unity*'s loaded with silk, saltpetre and indigo. She's sailing to Madagascar to join a China convoy bound for England."

Horne looked at the bull's hide map behind Watson's desk, seeing the shoe-shaped island of Madagascar positioned off the sloping east coast of Africa, southwest across the Indian Ocean from Bombay.

Watson said, "With that press gang out there, she'll probably want to be weighing anchor soon. Not even a Company ship is safe from those bastards." He turned to

Horne. "You and your men will travel as passengers as far as Madagascar. In Port Diego-Suarez, you go to Company House. Somebody there will give you your instructions."

"May I ask who, sir?"

"You'll find out soon enough." Watson turned back to the window.

"Yes, sir."

Watson was acting under orders from the Company's three Governors, Horne suspected, the men who directly controlled the Bombay Marine in the East India Company's hierarchy of power.

Moving behind his desk, the Commodore stood in front of his chair and looked down at the papers spread across the desk top. "So that's all I can tell you, Horne. Not why. Not when. Not where. Only that you're to sail to Madagascar. I'm sorry."

Realising he was being dismissed, Horne rose from his chair.

Watson began shuffling through the papers, head bent, saying in a lighter voice, "This war with France drags on, eh, doesn't it, Horne? It's been six months since the surrender of Pondicherry and still there's no word of any peace treaty."

"No, sir."

Watson shuffled more papers. "There's quarterdeck gossip that the French are about to mutiny on Mauritius if the frogs don't send them some wages."

"So I hear, sir."

Horne had indeed heard word about rebellion brewing amongst the French forces at their headquarters on the island of Mauritius. They had not been paid for almost a year.

Watson raised his eyes to Horne. "So France better dispatch some gold here pretty quickly."

"Yes, sir."

His gaze fixed on Horne, Watson asked, "But who knows, eh? Maybe a war chest's already at sea?"

"Very possibly, sir."

"That would be some prize to take, eh, Horne? A French war chest?"

"Yes, sir. By all means, sir."

"Whatever your mission, Horne, I know you'll do the Marine proud." Watson raised his arm, but the salute was lifeless, unenthusiastic.

Commodore Watson remained glumly at his desk after Adam Horne had left the chamber, wondering if he was allowing his brightest young captain to embark on a fatal course, putting Bombay Marines in unnecessary danger? Sitting under the slowly moving punkah fan, he reconsidered matters for what seemed to be the hundredth time.

The East India Company's three Governors—Spencer of Bombay, Pigot of Madras, Vansittart of Calcutta—had instructed Watson to dispatch Horne to Madagascar on the initial stage of a clandestine mission. The Governors had given Watson two brief details about the venture. The first was that the French government was sending a shipment of gold from France to Mauritius for the payment of long overdue wages to their colonial troops. The second fact was that the British Navy Board had heard of the French treasure ship and wanted the East India Company to commandeer the vessel after she rounded the Cape of Good Hope.

The Governors had unanimously agreed that Adam Horne's performance at Fort St. George made him the most eligible of the Marine's eleven captains to head the expedition and Watson had concurred with the Governors in their selection. Steely-minded, seemingly unafraid of death, Horne was also discreet and had an uncanny way of eluding the enemy. Furthermore, he had assembled and trained an oddly-assorted but strong support team which had survived the destruction of his ship, the *Eclipse*.

Watson's problem stemmed from the actual assigning of Horne to the mission. Not only had word of it come only two days ago, but it oddly circumscribed Watson's usual jurisdiction over his Marines. The Governors had empowered him to send Horne only as far as Port Diego-Suarez, the English post on Madagascar, insisting that they—or an agent of their choosing—would inform Horne about the nature of the mission upon his arrival.

Watson had argued that he should be the one to tell Horne. Apart from coming under his direct command, the dare-devil young Marine officer had a keen eye for strategy and could lend his knowledge to devising the plan of action in its early stages.

But the Governors had remained steadfast, refusing Watson's request to confide in Horne, and the Commodore, bowing to their authority, had agreed to send Horne and his squadron—cold, uninformed, ignorant of danger—on the first leg of their duty.

Watson had had similar experiences with the Company's Governors in the past, but they had always informed him on development, not totally excluded him as they were now doing.

How much was there to the mission that the Governors had not told him? Was commandeering the French war chest not its true objective? Was there some deeper plot which might tip the scales unfairly against Horne and his

Marines? Some reason which, if known to Watson, might make him loudly, firmly and vehemently protest against the mission?

Watson had answers to none of these questions; worse, he was ashamed of himself for not demanding answers. Why could he not have put himself—his job—on the line, insisting that the Governors tell him all they knew or terminate his own commission with the Honourable East India Company?

The answer was too shameful.

Before coming to Bombay, Watson had been Rear Admiral of the Blue in the West Indies. When the time for his retirement had arrived three years ago, the Honourable East India Company had invited him to become Commander-in-Chief of the Company's Bombay Marine. Watson, dreading life on a Dorset farm, had gratefully accepted the post in Bombay.

Sitting in his chamber high in Bombay Castle, he cursed himself for risking men's lives to protect his comforts and security. The attempt to warn Horne, to hint to him about the French war chest at the conclusion of the meeting, had been limp, weak, pathetic.

Oh, no, Watson thought miserably. This was no problem he could drown in his past panacea—gin. This would tear at his soul.

2

The Press Gang

Adam Horne left Bombay Castle through a small postern in the south wall. Emerging to the left of a goat pen, he made for an opening between two warehouses to avoid the bedlam of the marketplace. The silver and gold scabbard of his sabre jangled against his left leg as he walked at a brisk pace through the cool shade of the buildings. Irritated at Watson for not being able to supply details of the mission, he wondered why the old Commodore had mentioned a shipment of French gold before dismissing him. Was Watson concerned about a French mutiny? Would it affect the Marine? Coming to a junction of three passageways and momentarily uncertain which turning to take, Horne told himself to stop speculating about Watson's motives and concentrate on where he was going.

Eight years in Bombay had given Horne a reasonable knowledge of the city's many winding streets and narrow passageways. He had discovered that the best method of finding his way through the maze was to remember that the central point was Bombay Castle, that the bazaars, shops, houses, pagodas and temples spread out from the fortress like a fan across the marshy peninsula on which the city had been built.

Despite Bombay's cramped tenements and noisy streets, Horne preferred it to Madras or Calcutta. He liked the Moorish flavour created by red-tiled buildings crowding the bastions of Bombay Castle. He enjoyed living in a city which had no "Black Town" or "White Town" like Madras or Calcutta. The inhabitants here lived alongside one another—Indians, Africans, Europeans, Chinese—a stew of many nationalities which British colonials often found unappealing.

Reaching the bottom of the passageway, Horne came out at the top of the harbour. Fish nets were drying in the late morning sun and, beyond the wharf's edge, he could see native craft bobbing in the surf—Malabar sailing boats, snub-nosed fishing vessels, small rattan shells sewn with coir rope and tied at both ends like a child's toy. In the far distance, three merchant ships tipped at anchor near the harbour's wide mouth, their spars and rigging silhouetted against the hazy mountains on the mainland.

The *Unity* must be one of those Indiamen, he guessed. With the help of his spyglass he could study the ship on which he and his men would be sailing for Madagascar.

The thought that he would be a passenger and not captain dejected Horne. He pictured the *Eclipse*, imagining the excitement he would be feeling at this moment if he and his men were about to make way.

But no, it was indulgent to imagine what might have been. He had waited six months for an assignment. He now had one. He must be thankful for that fact and locate his men.

Climbing a steep incline of steps rising from the west

end of the wharf, he paused near the top to look one last time towards the sea. The wind was rising from the east, no finer day for sailing.

A Union Jack flapping on a brig caught his attention. Studying the Navy vessel, he guessed she must have brought the press gang into harbour to recruit men for His Majesty's Navy. Admiral Pocock's fleet must be hungry for seamen. The ocean air had weathered the brig's dark hull, giving her a sinister appearance, like a predator amongst the Indiamen in harbour, vessels which the press gang could board at any time of day or night and seize crew.

The Navy's press gang had the King's privilege to board any Company ship—as well as enter taverns, shops, even homes—to take men and boys to serve aboard Royal ships. It was no accident that members of a press gang were bullies, thugs, blackguards feared by everyone when they arrived in port.

The morning's sun was nearing its zenith when Horne knocked firmly on a small blue wooden door set within a crumbling white wall running along one side of a garbage-littered alley. A tiny brass grille was set in the middle of the door and, when Horne crooked his forefinger to rap a second time, the grille opened and a brown eye appeared on the far side of the delicate brasswork.

Horne bent forward to introduce himself but the grille slammed shut; iron bolts sounded on the far side of the door which swung open, and a man servant, wearing a white turban and a long white jacket, bowed deeply, gesturing for Horne to step from the alley.

Moving forward, Horne began to speak, but the servant hurriedly closed the door, beckoning him to follow.

Horne was surprised by the sharp contrast between the filthy alley and the beauty inside the high wall. Following the servant, he crossed a large garden planted with shrubs, flowers and fruit trees. Descending three flagstone steps, he came into a paved courtyard decorated with ornamental pools, bronze statues, and surrounded by arches of pink limestone.

A cry broke the garden's stillness.

Horne turned and saw another turbaned man—younger and shorter than the servant—running towards him.

"Captain sahib! Captain sahib!"

Horne grinned. It was Jingee.

Stopping a short distance from Horne, Jingee bent forward from the waist, salaaming and saying, "Welcome to my cousins' house, Captain sahib."

Horne accepted the greeting with a courteous nod, arms to his side.

He began, "I'm sorry to come unannounced, Jingee."

"I was expecting you, Captain sahib!"

Horne did not understand.

Jingee explained, "The astrologer told me to be prepared to embark on a long journey aboard a ship. I guessed that Commodore Watson must be giving us new orders, Captain sahib."

Indians of all castes visited astrologers for advice on health, travel, money or love. Horne was not surprised that Jingee, a member of the merchant class, the *Vaisya*, followed this popular Oriental habit.

He explained, "Commodore Watson has told us to be prepared to sail no later than tomorrow morning for Madagascar. We will be given further instructions there."

Jingee stood little more than five feet tall. His eyes were brown and shaped like almonds. His skin was a mellow umber, his complexion showing only a trace of a beard. In a voice which was thin but not effeminate, he said, "I am honoured to sail with you again, Captain sahib, wherever you lead us. I took an oath of allegiance to the Honourable East India Company and I have been waiting patiently to be called back into service. But it is to you, Captain sahib, that I am bonded. You took me from prison. You gave me a chance to prove I was no criminal but—" he held his small head high, "—a man of decency and honour."

Over the past six months, Horne had tried to meet the seven men from his squadron on a regular basis. But it was difficult keeping track of their day-to-day whereabouts, and he asked, "Jingee, can you help me find the others by this evening?"

"We can find them this afternoon, Captain sahib."

"Where should we start?"

"Kiro and Jud live beyond the Spice Market where you last saw them. Bapu still works in the Street of the Lanterns. He will be able to tell us where to find Babcock, Groot and Mustafa. They move around like nomads in the desert."

"Let's hope they don't move straight into the path of the press gang."

Jingee's eyes widened. "Yes, Captain sahib. My cousins told me about the press gang visiting the cattle yards. They are not starting in the waterfront as usual this trip. They are getting smarter." Jingee tapped the side of his turban.

"That's why we must hurry, Jingee."

"My cousins are not at home, Captain sahib. But they would be most displeased if I did not offer you hospitality before we left their house."

"Thank you, Jingee. But I'm certain your cousins would understand why we must not waste time sitting here drinking tea."

Jingee bowed. "As you wish, Captain sahib."

Horne glanced at the latticed arches behind Jingee. "As soon as you're ready, we can leave."

"But I *am* ready, Captain sahib! I have no uniform. No weapon. What else do I need? Nothing! I have already bidden my cousins goodbye this morning. As I said, Captain sahib, I was expecting you. In fact, you are a little late."

Jingee was one of Horne's most organised, most resourceful men. Accomplished as a cook, tailor, translator and guide, he was also surprisingly strong for his slight build, and masterful with a knife. Horne was glad to have the service again of the young Tamil's many diverse talents.

Jingee hurried to keep pace with Horne's brisk stride, explaining, as they passed through a narrow street lined with wooden tenements, that the last time he had seen Kiro and Jud was three days ago. Kiro was teaching the sons of rich families to duel like the ancient *Samurai* warriors of Japan, while Jud had found a job guarding treasures at a Hindu holy place, the Red Temple.

Emerging in a square where women in brightly dyed *saris* were gathered around a stone well, Jingee pointed to a narrow street which they must follow to find Kiro. Halfway across the square two dhooli-bearers rushed towards Horne, tugging at his coat sleeve and insisting that he ride on their palanquin, but Jingee waved his hand, scolding them in shrill Hindi as he led Horne to the far side of the square.

Dried palm fronds covered the street which climbed a low hill, the midday sun filtering through the loosely woven ceiling, giving a rich light to tradesmen standing or sitting cross-legged behind carpets spread on the ground.

This was the Spice Market, and a collection of seeds, pods, roots and fine powders were arranged in small piles or short rows in front of each pedlar, making the street aromatic with the pungent odours of cinnamon, cloves, nutmeg, turmeric and saffron.

As Horne and Jingee went further into the Spice Market, Horne noticed a young boy of eight or nine years following them along the dusty street, sometimes pushing his way ahead of them in the crowd. Horne did not mention the boy's presence to Jingee, wanting to see first if he might merely be a pedlar's scout.

As the street levelled at the top of the hill, the stalls of the spice merchants became interspersed with those of gem and precious metal dealers, turbaned men whose groundcloths were strewn with gold and silver jewellery hammered into a variety of designs, or a glittering array of garnets, pearls, rubies, sapphires and jade. Horne wondered how many of the stones were real and how many were sham, worth less than a nutmeg.

As they passed the last of the gem dealers, a pedlar fell in step with them, whispering in English, "Captain, you want to buy rubies?"

Jingee waved his hand. "Go away."

The pedlar was tall and broad-shouldered, and he persisted, "Captain, you want to buy the Grand Moghul's rubies?"

"Go away!" hissed Jingee.

"I give you my word," promised the pedlar. "These

rubies come from the royal city of Agra. From the Grand Moghul's *Diwan-i-am*."

Horne looked at the pedlar, a tall, black-skinned man with a white cloth pulled across the lower half of his face from the back of his turban, a black-and-brown-striped kaftan falling over his towering body.

Keeping pace with Horne, the pedlar lowered the cloth from his face, a big grin flashing a line of white teeth.

"Jud!"

Tall and thick-chested, Jud was an African from Oman with a face that looked as if it had been sculpted from ebony. He raised one arm in mock military salute, barking, "Captain Horne . . . *sir*!"

Horne replied with a quick snap of the arm.

All three men laughed.

Jingee, a midget alongside Jud, looked up at the African, explaining, "We were coming to find you in the Temple."

Jud shook his head. "Oh, you would not have found me at the Temple today, little friend. The priests heard about a press gang and decided I'd attract too much attention. They gave me these clothes and told me to lose myself in the bazaar."

Horne shook his head. "You'd be safer at sea, Jud."

"Say the word, Captain, and I'm ready."

"Tonight? Tomorrow?"

"Sir, you *are* serious!"

"Absolutely."

"The Company's assigned you a ship, sir?"

"Not yet, Jud. We sail as far as Madagascar on an Indiaman. We receive further instructions at Port Diego-Suarez."

Seeing a crowd collecting around them in the marketplace, Horne suggested, "Let's keep walking. I'll explain as we go."

The three men continued along the dusty street; the shops and stalls became fewer, being replaced by warehouses and sheds roofed with red tiles. The small native boy was still following them, Horne noticed, but he did not inform his companions about the tag-along child. Instead he proceeded to explain the plan to board the *Unity* between now and tomorrow morning's daybreak.

"Captain sahib, we are here." Jingee pointed at a pair of tall, iron-studded doors. "This is where Kiro meets his students."

Moving up to the doors, Jingee opened one with a slight push and stepped back for Horne and Jud to pass in front of him.

Beyond lay a great hall with a high ceiling covered with rattan. In the middle of the earth floor, two young boys, wooden poles gripped in both hands, were battling with one another, their feet dancing across the floor, the hollow clank of the poles echoing in the cavernous room.

Beside the boys moved Kiro, a sinewy Japanese in his mid-twenties, his black hair clipped short to his head, wearing a pair of long, wide white pants and a red band twisted round his forehead. Stepping from one leg to the other, he shouted, clapped his hands, whistled and grunted at the boys.

When he spotted the three visitors at the door, he motioned for the two students to continue without him, then crossed the dirt floor and bowed low to Horne, rising with a crisp military salute.

Horne returned the salute. "Excuse us for disturbing your class, Kiro."

Kiro looked quickly at the other two men and his tawny

face broke into a smile. "Sir, you come about a voyage?" he said.

Horne nodded. "We embark as soon as we find the others."

"Sir, I see Bapu every day." Kiro pointed to the street. "He still works at the elephant stables two streets away. And Babcock came here only this morning, to say that he, Groot and Mustafa are going to hide in a little house they found until the Navy's press gang leaves Bombay."

The European features of Babcock, Groot and Mustafa could easily attract the attention of a recruiting squad, Horne knew, much more easily than those of his other four men. Pleased to hear that they were taking steps to remain out of sight, he asked, "And you, Kiro? Are you safe here?"

Kiro smiled. "My students' fathers are rich shipbuilders, Captain Horne. They do not want their sons becoming common sailors. They have stationed spies around the city to warn me when a press gang is near. Look—" Kiro nodded to a shadowy corner. "There's Shashi, one of my little spies, over there."

Horne looked across to a far pillar and saw a young Indian peering out bashfully at them. It was the same boy whom he had seen following them in the bazaar.

Kiro explained, "I knew you were approaching before you arrived, sir. But because Shashi told me there was only one man in uniform, I did not become alarmed. I thought it—"

At that moment, one of the double doors burst open and a turbaned man rushed in from the street.

"Bapu!"

Bapu, an Indian from the northern district of Rajasthan, was taller than Jingee, broader chested, with a brawny body like the fabled warriors of the ancient caste to which he had been born, the *Kshatriya*.

Quickly saluting Horne, he gasped out, "We mustn't waste time, sir ... Our friends ... they're in trouble, sir ... Somebody's betrayed them and ... and the press gang's got them trapped in a house ... hurry ..."

Bapu disappeared out into the street.

With Jud and Jingee close behind, Horne and Bapu led the way down a sloping street, while Bapu continued his story. A neighbour had come to the elephant barn and told him that a spy had betrayed the whereabouts of his three friends to the Navy's press gang.

The afternoon heat had emptied the streets; only a few brown faces peered from behind closed shutters; the report of pistol shots sounded in the distance, and Bapu confirmed that they were approaching the location of the hideout. The echoing pop, pop, pop of weapons told Horne that the press gang had found Babcock, Mustafa and Groot, but the three Marines were obviously resisting them.

As they approached the intersection of two streets, Horne raised his hand and edged to the corner of a clay building. Removing his cocked hat, he peered down the adjoining street.

He was looking into a cul-de-sac. A cart had been over-turned three-quarters of the way down, to act as a barricade, and six men knelt behind it: two Royal Marines, a Royal Navy Lieutenant, two men whom Horne guessed to be British seamen and a slim Asian wearing a turban and long robe. The Marines and the Lieutenant were peering round the cart, their muskets pointing down the street, while the two seamen were behind the barricade, reloading their flintlocks with ball and powder. Beyond them, Horne saw a small house at the end of the street; it had no windows, only a squat door and reed walls which immediately impressed him as being highly inflammable.

Surveying the rest of the street, he pulled back his head and levelled the hat over his forehead. "There are six of them," he reported. "They've barricaded the house with a cart. But they aren't too concerned about covering themselves from the rear."

Anxiously, Bapu asked, "Any sign of activity in the house, sir?"

"None I can see."

Jingee whispered, "Can we sneak up on the Navy men, Captain sahib, and—" He mimed slitting his throat.

Horne shook his head. "Not with their firearms, Jingee. It'd be too risky." Turning to Bapu, he asked, "Is there a back entrance to small houses like that?"

Bapu knew the house and replied without hesitation. "No, sir. It's called a *howdah*, like a *howdah* on the back of an elephant. But instead of four curtains, its walls are grass and wood."

"Which burn."

Bapu looked at the others. "I'm afraid so, sir. The heat of one musket ball could set it ablaze."

The men exchanged glances.

By now Kiro, shirtless and wearing only his white Japanese trousers, had joined the group. "There are five of us, sir," he said. "We can cross by the roof tops and drop down on the wagon from both sides."

Horne had taken that and other facts into consideration. But apart from being worried about fire, he was also concerned that his men might become too enthusiastic in a rescue attempt. Their loathing of press gangs—coupled with the anticipation of a long-awaited reunion—could easily intoxicate them and turn what should be a minor venture into a wild, excessive blood bath.

"We must remember that if we kill one of them, we've got a price on our heads," he cautioned. "They're the King's men, for better or worse." Turning to Bapu, he asked, "Can you get horses where you work?"

"Four, sir."

"Fetch them."

Before Bapu could move, there was a sudden lull in the shooting. Horne removed his cocked hat and leaned round the corner again. He quickly withdrew his head.

Keeping his back to the wall, he whispered, "Two men are coming this way. One's a Marine. The other's Indian. Bapu, look and tell me if you recognise him."

Bapu dropped to the ground and peered round the base of the wall. Rising to his feet, he stood beside Horne, saying, "Aye, I know him, sir. The dirty *Sudra*'s name is Rangi. He hangs around wharfside taverns. There's no doubt about it, sir. He's probably the one who betrayed their hideout."

"Get the horses, Bapu. Bring them back here."

When Bapu had departed, Horne began explaining the first steps of his hurriedly improvised plan to the other three men.

"Kiro, you come with me."

The Japanese moved to Horne's side.

Looking from Jud to Jingee, Horne continued, "There's an alleyway halfway down the street. You two wait here. Don't move until you see Kiro and me go into the alleyway. Understand?"

"Aye, aye, sir," nodded Jud.

"Aye, aye, Captain sahib," whispered Jingee.

Horne beckoned to Kiro. "Let's go."

Resettling the cocked hat on his head, he rounded the corner and walked authoritatively toward the two approaching men. Kiro followed a few steps behind him.

The Royal Marine halted when he saw Horne's gold-faced uniform. Touching the base of his tall shako hat, he reported, "Men resisting the King's forces here, Captain."

Pleased for once that his frock-coat so closely resembled the Royal Navy's uniform, Horne continued walking towards the Royal Marine, speaking in a firm but low voice so as not to alert the men kneeling behind the cart.

He demanded, "Who's in charge, Sergeant?"

The Marine began to reply but Horne's left arm flew at him, striking his chin. Using the ancient Greek method of open-hand fighting, he cut his other hand into the man's chest and neck. Kiro used *Karate* to attack the Indian spy, knocking him unconscious with three deft chops.

Seeing Horne and Kiro pull the two men into the alleyway, Jingee and Jud raced towards them, pulling off belts and turbans to gag and bind the two victims.

The four friends quickly tied the men's hands and feet, then Horne whispered, "Jud, you come with Kiro and me. Jingee, you wait here until you see it's clear to make a dash for the house." Readjusting his hat, smoothing his shirt and frock-coat he stepped from the alley, followed by Kiro and Jud.

As they approached the wagon, he was amused to see that the attack had not attracted the attention of the other men. Moving closer, he demanded in a loud voice, "Who's in charge here?"

The Naval officer jumped at the sound of Horne's voice. Seeing the gold-braided uniform, he sprang to his feet and saluted. "Lieutenant Fanshaw, sir!"

Horne's hand caught Fanshaw's chin as he kicked a flintlock from the next man's grip. Kiro tackled a seaman loading a musket as Jud charged the fourth man.

Behind them, Jingee dashed from the alley, raced round the overturned wagon and ran for the grass house, shouting, "Babcock! Groot! Mustafa! Open the door!"

The small door flew open; three men bolted stoop-shouldered from the hut: Groot wearing a blue cap pushed back on his blond head; Mustafa, his hirsute chest bare and his thick, black, Turkish moustache lifted in a rare grin; Babcock with his sandy hair tousled and his ears large and red.

As Horne helped Kiro and Jud to drag the four remaining men of the press gang from the wagon to the hut, Babcock ran to Horne shouting, "Holy hell! It's about time you got here, Horne! These two were driving me crazy! Groot talks too much and Mustafa doesn't talk enough!"

Horne tossed the Lieutenant's unconscious body into the hut and called to the big American colonial, "Babcock, you still haven't learned how to address an officer properly, have you?"

"Yes ... *suh!*" mocked Babcock, throwing out his chest.

A rumble sounded in the distance. Turning, the men saw Bapu rounding the corner on a black stallion, leading three other horses by their reins.

3

The *Unity*

The Arabian Sea sprayed Adam Horne with fine pin-points of mist as he stood at the larboard rail of the Honourable East India Company's Indiaman, the *Unity*, five hundred ton burden, on its southwest course.

Booted feet wide apart, chest bared for work, he bellowed to the five men climbing three ropes he had ordered to be hung from the main topgallant yardarm. The second day since weighing anchor, it was the first occasion for Horne to test his Marines' stamina.

Hands cupped to his mouth, he trumpeted, "Mustafa, too slow! Bapu, you move like one of your elephants! Climb like a monkey, man! Climb like a monkey! Keep your legs wrapped around that rope, Jingee! If you fall, you'll burn your hands!"

Horne was not surprised that Jud led the rope climb. No wall had been too high for the African to scale before he had been captured and imprisoned for thievery. Horne remembered how Jud's criminal background had helped him become a good topman aboard the *Eclipse*.

Bapu and Kiro moved up the two ropes flanking Jud, the roll of the ship causing them to swing back-and-forth from the fore to the mizzen mast. Both men wore white *dhotis*; both had knotted rags around their foreheads, the sinewy Japanese looking as dark as the brawny Indian.

Behind them moved Jingee and Mustafa. Horne watched Jingee struggling to climb hand-over-hand as the ship's movement swung him like a pendulum against the billowing topgallant sail. He noticed, too, that Mustafa— heavily muscled, a true personification of the legendary barrel-chested Turk—seemed to be slowed by his bulk.

Groot and Babcock were not taking part in the morning drill. When the *Unity* had got under way the day before, the ocean's dips and swells had sent them vomiting to the scuppers and had incapacitated them again today in their berths. Horne knew it was not unusual for a man to lose his sea legs after spending a considerable length of time ashore, but he was surprised it had happened to men as seasoned as Babcock and Groot. Hoping that they were not suffering from a more serious complaint, he consoled himself that they were merely passengers on this section of the voyage.

The *Unity*'s Captain, Thomas Goodair, had cordially welcomed Horne aboard the Indiaman two days ago. He had not asked why Bombay Marines should be sailing as passengers aboard a merchant ship instead of patrolling coastlines and compiling charts, performing their customary duties.

Nothing about this mission was going to be ordinary, Horne had decided. He had the inexplicable feeling that events would continue as unconventionally as they had begun.

Having galloped from the district beyond the Spice

Market where they had left the press gang bound and gagged, Horne had ordered his men to abandon their horses near South Wharf. Seizing a fisherman's *dongi*, they had rowed across the harbour to the *Unity*, announcing themselves with a loud shout before climbing a rope ladder to the port entry.

Fortunately, Captain Goodair had been aboard, reading Commodore Watson's letter informing him of Horne's imminent arrival with seven Marines. An Englishman with a kind face weathered by thirty-seven years in Indian Service, he had assigned the Great Cabin to Horne and had invited him to dine with him in his cabin. The other men were assigned to sleep with the crew below the forecastle, and to eat with them between the guns fore of the main deck. Goodair, as anxious as Horne to escape the press gang, had weighed anchor at first light of the new day.

His eyes raised aloft, Horne backed towards the forecastle as he saw Jud—followed by Kiro—swing from the yardarm, snatch for the ratlines, and begin scrambling down, down, down past the shrouds.

Watching Kiro gaining on Jud, he pulled off his boots to participate in the next drill, and as the two men—Kiro now in the lead—cleared the futtock shrouds, he bellowed, "Jump!"

Kiro hit deck a few seconds before Jud.

"Take . . . *cover*!"

Horne dived as he shouted the command, leading Kiro and Jud to the narrow space he had created by weaving the ship's lifelines with auxiliary ropes and stretching them starboard to larboard.

Cheek pressed to the deck, he propelled himself by his elbows, scrambling towards the capstan. The smell of tar—mixed with the holystone's pungency—filled his nostrils. Conserving his breath as he crawled, Horne was glad he had followed a daily regimen of exercise and food over the past six months, performing the circuit of routines he had learned long ago from an old British soldier, Elihu Cornhill, at a tumbledown estate in Wiltshire. Many military critics denigrated Cornhill's survival techniques as eccentric, even dangerous. Horne had learned that they saved men's lives.

Bapu, a hefty man with skin the colour of rich earth and eyes placed closely together like a snake, knew he was no sailor. He was a soldier. A warrior. A bandit. So why did he feel so satisfied to be back at sea, sweating out his guts in the midday sun?

Neither was Bapu a follower, an acolyte, someone to be part of another man's pack. Born a *Kshatriya* leader, he had been a renegade chieftain to a band of cut-throats in the Rajasthan hills before being apprehended and imprisoned at Bombay Castle. With that history, why was he so damnably content at being reunited with Captain Horne? Why had he spent the past six months in a Bombay elephant house, living no better than some lowly *mahoot*, waiting for Horne to snap his fingers for him to come running?

These questions occurred to Bapu in fragments as he bellied across deck, climbed ratlines, charged a musket's bayonet towards the straw-filled dummy fixed to the forecastle, Horne shouting orders like a master.

Having been plucked by Horne from a subterranean prison, Bapu was grateful for being saved from a life of incarceration, but his gratitude to Horne did not include devotion. He did not *worship* Horne; he had seen enough of the Englishman to know that the *topiwallah* was no god.

Meeting at beer shops. Swimming to Elephant Rock. Gathering for suppers. Bapu had seen Horne, alone and with the other six Marines, during the past land-locked months in Bombay. During that time, he had observed how uneasy Horne was on land, restless, a man with nowhere to go, a man with little to talk about—or, at least, a man not willing to share private thoughts.

Horne was a strong man. Bapu had also seen that when Horne became angry, his face looked like the head of a hound ready to attack. Instead of depending on strong jaws and teeth to tear into his victim, Horne threw his whole body—including his mind—towards attack. Horne's ambition seemed to be to teach other men to fight in a similar way.

Perhaps that's why Bapu admired Horne. Horne shared; he was one of the most generous men Bapu had ever met, not only with objects, but with time, ideas, accomplishments. Was that not the true test of generosity in a man?

Apart from meeting Horne in the past months, Bapu and the other six Marines had grouped together for their own reunions. Groot, Mustafa and Babcock had even shared rooms. Bapu knew that some people believed he was probably a closer friend to Jingee than to the other Marines because they were both Indian. But Bapu considered Jingee to be like many men of the *Vaisya* caste— arrogant, demanding, overly ambitious.

Belonging to the older, more superior Hindu caste of the *Kshatriya*, Bapu was supposedly superior to someone of the *Vaisya* caste—even Jingee admitted that. Bapu thought that perhaps that was the reason Jingee expected him to lead a superior life, aspire to the grandeur of elite forebears, not live in an elephant house like some *Sudra mahoot*, a man below the caste system.

Bapu's closest friend ashore had been Kiro. His background as a Japanese pirate had been close to Bapu's own past as a bandit. They had swapped stories, laughingly entertained future plans. Bapu liked Kiro because he was never loud, never brash, always showing a serene face to the world, except when he became angry, and then, Kiro exploded with the wrath of the *Samurai* he was.

Bapu guessed that he and Kiro were friends because they had both forsaken their illustrious birthrights as heirs to an ancient warrior tradition. Could they somehow placate their ancestors by excelling as Bombay Marines?

What did the future hold as a Bombay Marine? Or would Bapu return to hill life in northern India? He believed that if he did revert to a bandit's life, he would return a better man than when he had been taken away in chains. Horne had improved Bapu's strength, sharpened his intelligence, made his eye keener.

Since leaving Bombay aboard the *Unity*, Horne had said nothing about their new mission except that the Marines would receive their orders on arrival in Madagascar. Bapu lay awake at night wondering what the assignment would be. Would it prove to be worth the lowly life he had led during the past months, living, waiting, biding his time in an elephant's shed?

He suspected he would not be disappointed. Horne was a *feringhi*, a foreigner, but he also belonged to the warrior caste. By nature.

Fatigued by the sea air and the first day of rigorous drill circuits, Adam Horne looked forward to an evening alone in the Great Cabin. His hopes were destroyed, however, when Captain Goodair sent an invitation to join him for supper in the ship's roundhouse. Horne knew he must not decline the offer.

Roast fowl and potatoes cooked in the Indian oil called *ghee*, served with an assortment of hot and sweet relishes and pickles, composed the modest but pleasant supper. The table servant produced bowls of fresh fruit and an assortment of sweet biscuits along with the port.

The *Unity* crested on the ocean's swells, creaking down into the next trough. Captain Goodair was talking about a merchant ship's deceptive appearance. Generous with his wine, he refilled Horne's bumper from the cut-glass decanter and said, "A new Indiaman isn't as large as ships in the last century. When too many leviathans came home empty-bellied from the East, owners began trimming down their size.

"Although they're built like warships, these new ships are not as strong as they appear. The *Unity* looks like a ship of seventy-four guns when, in actual fact, she's equipped with twenty-eight, and those are spread along the upper deck. You've probably noticed the lower ports are caulked shut with pitch and oakum."

Horne had indeed seen that the Indiaman's lower gunports had been sealed shut. Wanting to confirm his suspicions as to the reason, he asked, "Sir, who ordered them shut?"

"Percival Sidwell. The ship's husband."

There were powerful businessmen called "husbands" who managed all aspects of an Indiaman, including its "bottom" privileges—the right to replace the ship with a new vessel in future years. Horne knew from past experience that a ship's husband worried more about profits than a ship's fighting power.

As if reading Horne's thoughts, Goodair said, "Military men disagree with the elimination of guns for cargo. But, then, you probably think we should boast our own Marine unit, too!"

Indiamen carried no Marines like a Navy ship, leaving the ship's defence to its crew, the incentive to fight being the Company's rule: A crew loses all claim on wages if a ship is captured.

Horne saw no reason to raise old arguments and spoil a relaxing evening. Instead, he voiced one of the East India Company's main disputations against the need for heavy arms on a merchantman. "Soon you'll be in convoy, sir, and have the safety of numbers."

"Aye, we'll be fourteen strong for England."

Satisfied with the tasty meal and pleasant conversation, Horne pursued a subject he guessed Goodair might enjoy with his bumper of port.

"Who do you consider to be an Indiaman's most formidable enemy at sea, Captain?"

Goodair considered the question as he fingered crumbs on the table's damask cloth. "In these waters, the chieftains from the Malabar Coast are our biggest worry, Horne, those successors to that old pirate, Angria, whom the Bombay Marines chased from his lair."

Horne had sailed with the previous Bombay Marine Commander-in-Chief, Commodore James, aboard James's flagship, the *Protector*, forty-four guns, on the raid of Angria's stronghold. It had been Commodore James who had raised Horne to the rank of Captain after that victory.

He asked, "And who, sir, is your most dangerous foe the closer you sail to Madagascar? Passing from the Arabian down into the Indian Ocean?"

Goodair answered without hesitation. "Those damned

raiders from Dar es Salaam. Worse than privateers from Oman, in my estimation."

Horne repeated another popular opinion. "But many privateers are intimidated by the size of an Indiaman, by her close resemblance to one of His Majesty's warships."

"True, true. But you know yourself, Horne, that all pirates are bully boys, ready to tackle anything." Resettling himself in his chair, he confided, "The sad fact is that pirates in the Arabian Sea have grown rich off Company pickings. The devils are able now to buy frigates from the same dockyards in Bombay that are building merchant ships for the Company."

From the subject of pirates, Goodair moved onto discussing crew, mentioning the illness of his First Mate, Charles Ames, whom he had confined to quarters with a fever, hoping to prevent panic spreading about possible contagion. He also questioned Horne about himself, showing particular interest in the fact that Horne's father was a banker, especially since the Horne Bank in London was located in Lombard Street, only five streets away from Leadenhall Street, the headquarters of the Honourable East India Company.

"I shall call in at the bank and offer my respects to your father," he said, "when I go up to London to make my report to the Committee. Perhaps you have a letter I can deliver."

Horne seized on the offer. "I was planning a letter in Bombay and should be most grateful, sir, if you would carry it back to England."

Goodair's offer also provided Horne with an excuse to take his leave from the roundhouse. Begging permission to retire to his cabin and write his letter, he bade Goodair goodnight, thanking him again for allowing the Bombay

Marines to train aboard the *Unity* on their voyage to Madagascar.

Alone in the Great Cabin, Horne sat at his desk, listening to the slapping of the waves in the night.

Watching the yellow light from the brass lamp dance across the blank writing sheet, he considered how he should start his father's letter. Deciding to begin with an introductory note about Captain Goodair's generous offer to deliver the communication, he reached for the inkwell.

A knock sounded on the cabin door.

Hoping that the late-night caller might be Babcock or Groot coming to report an improvement in health, Horne sprung from the chair and pulled back the bolt.

In the companionway stood the *Unity*'s Second Mate, a buck-toothed young man named Simon Tree.

"Sorry to disturb you, Captain Horne, sir. But I saw a light under your door and thought I might have a few words with you."

Stepping back to allow the merchant ship's young officer to enter the cabin, Horne, said, "Yes. Of course. Come in," adding quickly, "for a few moments, Mr. Tree."

"Thank you, sir."

Tree entered the cabin, carrying his cocked hat, his sandy brown hair pulled into a queue, his weak chin descending to a prominent Adam's apple.

Horne pointed to the chair by the writing desk. "I can't offer you any refreshment, Mr. Tree. I boarded rather hurriedly and had no time to collect any provisions."

Tree's laugh was loud, coarse, like a mule's bray. "We *saw* you board, sir! Was somebody chasing you?"

Horne chose to ignore both his visitor's laughter and

the questions. He wanted neither to hear nor to add to quarterdeck gossip about himself and his men. It was no secret that the Maritime Service held the Bombay Marine in contempt. Horne guessed that the *Unity* abounded with rumours about the reason he was sailing to Madagascar with his men, not to mention their unorthodox arrival.

Tree said, "I'm sorry to hear about your two Marines being ill, Captain Horne. Are they feeling better?"

Was the ship's officer mocking Babcock and Groot for being sea-sick? Or had the Second Mate actually come here at this late hour to offer sympathy? Horne doubted it.

"You probably know, sir," Tree continued, "that the First Mate is ill, too. Quite a bit more seriously than your men, sir."

"So I understand, Mr. Tree." Horne was surprised that Tree should speak so freely about his superior officer.

Tree's lips lifted into a smile. "You don't remember me, do you, sir?"

The question caught Horne unawares. "Remember you, Mr. Tree? From where?"

"London, sir. My family moved to your neighbourhood the year you went to study in Wiltshire. I was only ten years old but I remember you clearly."

Horne studied the chinless officer more closely, suspecting that he was like many privileged young men he remembered from London—opinionated, none too tactful, relatively harmless if you ignored their abrasive manner.

Moving to the edge of his chair, Simon Tree enthused, "Sir, you were everybody's hero in the neighbourhood, especially when Elihu Cornhill accepted you into his school."

"You lived near Mount Street?"

"Park Street."

Horne recalled no family by the name of Tree in Park Street, or any other street near his family's Mayfair house.

Tree added, "And this morning when I saw you training your men, I wondered if you'd learned all those hops and jumps and rope swings at Cornhill's school. I've heard how that old man taught chaps to leap about with swords and muskets day and night."

Horne admired inquisitive people, but not when their questions were directed at him. Especially when the questions involved subjects which he closely guarded, such as his precious years studying with Elihu Cornhill.

Oblivious of Horne's failure to reply to his question, Tree continued, "You joined the Bombay Marine around that time, didn't you, sir? When your fiancée was killed? Wasn't your young lady stabbed to death in Covent Garden, sir?"

The statement stunned Horne; the facts were true but, hearing a stranger blurt them out so unexpectedly, so callously, made Horne pull himself up ramrod stiff on his chair.

Tree saw that he had offended Horne and lowered his eyes. "Sir, I'm sorry," he apologised. "Forgive me, sir. I've overstepped my bounds. I got excited by actually talking to you after all these years. I've always admired you, sir, and—" He raised both large red hands, repeating, "I'm truly sorry, sir. The last thing I'd want to do is offend you, sir."

Touched by the raw sincerity in Tree's voice, Horne considered that the spoiled young Londoner might have another facet to him, that apart from his offensive manner he possessed a pup-like devotion to superiors.

Softening, he asked, "Did we actually know one another, Mr. Tree?"

"No, sir. Not as friends, sir. You were much older than me."

"Hmmm. Of course."

Horne decided to ask a few questions of his own. "Why did you join the Company's Maritime service, Mr. Tree?" he began.

Sitting on the edge of his chair, Tree regained his former enthusiasm. "There are five sons in our family, sir. My eldest brother—that's Jonathan—he went into Father's hostelry business. The next is Roderick; he entered the Ministry. I'm the third son. I decided I'd better join the Service before my younger brother—he's Clarence— or else I'd have to join the Navy."

"And you wouldn't want that."

"The Navy?" Missing the note of sarcasm in Horne's words, Tree blurted, "Sir, I'd rather join the Bombay Marine."

Horne's voice remained calm. "Tell me, Mr. Tree," he asked, "why you have such a . . . low opinion of the Bombay Marine?"

Tree's baby-smooth skin flushed a deep scarlet as he realised what he had said. "Sir, you must excuse me," he mumbled, fidgeting in his seat, "I didn't intend offence to you, sir."

"Please, Mr. Tree. Please. Speak. I'm a Marine. I want to hear why an ambitious young man like yourself chose the Maritime Service over the Bombay Marine."

"But, sir, you're not like other Marines, sir."

"What makes you say that, Mr. Tree?"

"Why, you're . . . you're educated, sir. You're intelligent. You're . . ."

Horne enjoyed watching the gangling young man squirm. "Are you saying, Tree, that most Marines are oafs? Ignorant, thick-head louts whom you wouldn't want to be associated with?"

"No, sir. Of course not, sir."

The shuffle of feet sounded outside the cabin.

Horne raised one hand for silence.

Tree whispered, "Sir, what is it?"

Horne did not reply, listening instead to the waves crashing against the Indiaman's hull, the sound of wind singing through the rigging ropes, and, finally, in the distance, the hail which he thought he had heard, a distant voice calling, "Sail ho! Sail ho!"

Forgetting he was a passenger, not the captain, on the *Unity*, Horne grabbed for his sabre.

Captain Goodair stood on the windward side of the quarterdeck and, handing his spyglass to Horne, said, "The moon's bright enough to see her topgallants."

Peering through the spyglass, Horne saw a small, glowing shape on the southern horizon, a white triangle brilliant against the night's steely sky. Thinking she might be a merchant ship, he swept the sea with the spyglass to see if she was sailing in convoy.

"Nothing there, Horne."

Captain Goodair's abrupt words told Horne he had overstepped his mark. Returning the spyglass, he moved back, allowing Goodair to enjoy the prerogative of an Indiaman's captain—of pacing the quarterdeck's windward side.

Goodair snapped shut the glass and called, "Mr. Tree?"

"Aye, aye, sir?"

"We're a good distance from the vessel, Tree, but we do not want to lose our advantage."

"No, sir."

"Pass orders to bear-up, Tree."

"Aye, aye, sir."

"And get Ames up here," he called after him.

Turning to execute Goodair's command, Tree descended the steps to the main deck and soon men were running to the sheets, scurrying along the rigging in the glow of a full moon.

From the mainmast came another hail. "Sail ahoy! Sail to larboard! Sail ahoy!"

Goodair snapped open the spyglass and scanned the distant horizon, pausing to hold the glass on one spot a few minutes, before finally handing it to Horne.

Horne moved to Goodair's side; he sighted a second ship, smaller than the first, but judging from the way it was bearing down on the Indiaman, he guessed that both vessels were prowling together for rich prizes and had evidently decided their search had ended with the *Unity*.

4

The Eagle and the Kingfisher

Captain Goodair trained his spyglass on the distant frigate. "She's got the weather gauge."

Horne pulled his coat around him as a roller crashed against the *Unity*'s poop, its spray breaking across the quarterdeck, disintegrating into small, silver beads in the early morning darkness.

Sweeping the spyglass to the smaller vessel, Goodair studied her for a few moments before saying, "The small one—by Jove, yes—she's a pattimar!"

Pattimars were India's best sailing craft in Horne's estimation, wooden vessels measuring over seventy feet in length, using nuts and bolts in the European manner rather than being sewn with coconut rope like so many Oriental boats. A large, raked foresail gave the sturdy ship an exotic, almost jaunty appearance—and excellent manoeuvrability.

Despite his fascination with pattimars, Horne looked back to the frigate off the larboard beam, remembering Goodair's remark at supper about Arab raiders buying frigates from Bombay shipbuilders. He knew there could be no better ship for hit and run attacks than a sleek, three-masted vessel. He wondered, though, if pirates from Africa's west coast would wander so far up into the Arabian Sea. Or were raiders becoming more adventurous in their newly commissioned European-style ships? Also, might troublesome war chiefs from south of Bombay also be sailing in frigates, venturing out farther than the Malabar Coast?

The fact that a frigate and pattimar were prowling together in search of booty also intrigued Horne. He smiled at the idea of such an unlikely paired team, predators large and small, like an eagle and a kingfisher.

How long had they been following the *Unity*? Had they been circling, those two birds of prey, waiting for the clouds to clear from the full moon so that they could close in for the kill? Had the frigate and pattimar spotted the *Unity* by chance, or were they acting on some tip from port, from a spy who had spoken of the merchantman's rich cargo? Or perhaps they were more interested in the ship's munitions and hardware. They might also have a pact with France, be French allied privateers.

Horne's speculations were disturbed when he heard Tree mounting the quarterdeck ladder, taking three rungs at a time, apparently forgetting the Maritime Service's pretensions to ape the protocol of His Majesty's Navy.

Goodair asked, "You found Mr. Ames?"

Touching his hat, Tree reported between quick gulps for air. "Sir . . . Mr. Shanks regrets that . . . there's no possibility that . . . Mr. Ames can attend you, sir . . . because—"

Tree glanced at Horne.

"Because why, man?"

Tree bit his lower lip, looking young, frightened, and—Horne was sorry to admit—oafish.

"Speak up, man!" ordered Goodair, a stern father speaking to an awkward son.

"It's fever, sir. The First Mate is—" Tree's voice lowered. "Mr. Shanks has had to tie Ames in his hammock, sir. The First Mate is . . . delirious."

Goodair lowered his head, closing his eyes.

Horne remained silent, oblivious of the sea spray as he thought about the ship's lanky surgeon, Ronald Shanks. He had met Shanks for the first time yesterday when he had enquired after Babcock and Groot. Unlike many ship's surgeons whom he had encountered, Shanks had not appeared to be a drunkard, but neither had he struck him as a notably efficient man.

A blast sounded beyond the larboard beam. Horne jerked his head in time to see a puff of smoke rise form the frigate's gun ports.

Goodair did not lift the spyglass to study the approaching frigate. He stood with both hands gripped behind his back and, ignoring Tree, asked, "Captain Horne, would you judge that to be a ranging shot?"

"Yes, sir. Most certainly, sir." Horne was amused by the wry way Captain Goodair referred to him for an opinion; the Merchant Commander included him in this encounter as casually as if it were merely an extension of the supper's conversation.

Goodair nodded. "One thing's certain. Whoever those dogs are, they certainly can't be intending that blast as a warning for us to—" he snorted, "surrender ourselves to them."

"No, sir. I wouldn't say they intend that, sir." Horne stopped himself from adding that the ranging shot was good reason to consider the unmarked ship an enemy and to begin making preparations for battle.

Holding one hand behind his frock-coat, Goodair extended the other, palm upward, to Tree, requesting, "My speaking trumpet, Mr. Tree."

"Aye, aye, sir."

In a minute, Tree returned, handing Goodair his gleaming mouthpiece, eyes darting to the frigate quickly closing the gap of choppy waves between herself and the *Unity*.

Goodair accepted the trumpet from Tree like a gentleman receiving some trifling object from his major-domo in the hallway of his home, and ordered in a calm, assured voice, "Clear for action, Mr. Tree."

"Aye, aye, sir." Tree touched his hat.

"Run out the guns."

"Aye, aye, sir."

Tree turned, glancing nervously at Horne as he crossed to the companion ladder. The young man's uneasy excitement contrasted sharply with Goodair's calm, almost blasé preparations for battle.

In a short time, the *Unity*'s deck was sanded, pails of water placed by the guns, the ginger-whiskered gunner, Ben Warner, and his men having wrapped bandannas around their ears as protection against the blast of the eighteen pounders.

Listening to the snap of sails, Horne wondered where his men were at this moment. By custom, passengers should be confined to their quarters in battle. Trusting that they were prepared to be called for action if necessary, he turned his attention back to the enemy.

Beyond the *Unity*'s larboard bow, the frigate was cutting across the silver-capped sea in the harsh moonlight, her wind-filled royals and topgallants in clear view as she bore down to deliver—Horne guessed—her first blast to the Indiaman. He could not help but admire the ship's majesty, remembering the frigate of his own command, the *Eclipse*.

Raising his eyes aloft, he saw that Goodair was keeping the Indiaman as near to the wind as she would lie, the rigging singing, the sails snapping, on a course to parallel the frigate.

Horne wondered whether the pirate captain—if, indeed, that was what he was—had noticed yet that the Indiaman's lower gun ports were not open. Or did he know—had been informed—that they had been caulked shut for cargo?

Goodair appeared to be undaunted by his lack of gun power; continuing on the opposite tack to the frigate, the waves hissing around him, he was apparently waiting for his own moment to fire.

As the two vessels approached prow to prow, Goodair slowly, confidently raised his trumpet to his mouth, calling, "Starboard . . . fire!"

The Indiaman shook as the guns belched flames in the darkness.

Seeing the aim fall short of target, Horne was surprised to observe that no smoke arose from the pirate's guns. They had not fired—why? Had they judged the distance too great? They had been right. Horne wondered if they were better seamen than Goodair.

As the *Unity*'s gunner called the guns to be run in, Goodair began orders to put the ship around, commencing, "Put the wheel hard over!"

Horne, intrigued with the merchant captain's manœuvre, waited for the bow to begin slowly turning.

After the headsail sheets and bowlines were placed,

tacks and sheets hauled, Goodair called for the wheel to come hard over, and as the Indiaman turned in the wind, Horne thought how effortless the gesture seemed, and how calmly, almost with detachment, the captain was conducting himself in the operation. Was it so easy for him? Or was he always so disinterested and detached?

Realising he had been holding his breath, Horne glanced towards the frigate and saw her bow cutting the waves, changing tack to parallel the *Unity* yet again. He remembered the eagle's companion, the kingfisher, and looked over his shoulder; the pattimar had also tacked and was moving directly towards the *Unity*'s stern.

Goodair had also spotted the pattimar's raked sail filled with wind and called, "Prepare larboard guns."

As the gunner's men laboured the guns into position, Horne began to suspect the pirates' intentions: the frigate had been used to bait the *Unity*, to lead her into the tack: when the Indiaman had responded and tacked, the pattimar moved in for what was to appear as a surprise attack from another angle. But during the fleeting minutes in which the *Unity* was preparing to divert that aggression from the pattimar, the frigate would give the true death blow.

As the grim realisation dawned that the frigate was double-guessing them, Horne turned to see how far she was abeam. At the same moment, a blast filled the air, timbers crashed nearby and he was thrown off his feet.

Captain Goodair knew that his history in service to the Honourable East India Company was sound but not heroic, that he was more of a merchant than a fighting man. Fifty-three years old, he was proud that his ship had never spent idle years in port like many other Indiamen. The majority of the Company's eighty-eight ships stayed one year in three in England.

Franklin Goodair had begun service as Second Mate aboard the *Duke of Harrow*. By his third voyage to India, he had risen to First Mate aboard the *Unity*. On a voyage freighted from Bantam, the *Unity*'s Captain had died from fever and Goodair brought ship and cargo safely home. The ship's husband—along with the Captain's widow—agreed that young Franklin Goodair should be rewarded both for delivering the *Unity* and for bringing a handsome profit home from the voyage. Offering him command of the ship, they made provisions for him to pay for the privilege from his profits over future trips to the Orient.

Having command of an Indiaman was like owning highly valuable property; a captain could buy it, sell it, settle it on heirs, but, above all, share in a voyage's profits.

Rich from his seventeen years as Captain and Commander of HEIC *Unity*, Goodair had also secured a social position for himself and his family. In Bath, they associated with the aristocracy, enjoyed a houseful of servants, a walled garden, carriages and frequent trips to London. It was in India, however, that Goodair enjoyed the full benefit of his status as Captain and Commander. Whenever the *Unity* entered port, there was a salute of guns. Guards turned out when Goodair entered—and departed from—Bombay Castle, or any of the other Company's foreign fortresses. His name was always included on the invitation lists at Government House.

Goodair took a quick inventory of all these worldly achievements as he stood on the *Unity*'s quarterdeck, seeing smoke rise from the pirate guns trained on his ship and knowing there was nothing he could do to escape the bombardment.

"Captain Goodair? Captain Horne? Are you hit?"

Tree's frantic calls came from beyond the quarterdeck ladder as Horne hurriedly lifted planks and pulled rigging from Goodair's mangled body, hoping to find him alive.

The enemy had struck the poopdeck, bombarding Goodair with a hail of flying splinters, piercing his chest, arms and legs. Kneeling beside his blood-covered body, Horne saw his chest moving and realised with relief that he was still breathing, he was not dead.

Sending Tree for the surgeon and his mate, he pulled away shreds of the spanker sail from Goodair's boots, cut the rope dangling across his gaping red wounds, and stepped back as Tree returned with the other two men.

As Shanks the surgeon eased Goodair onto a stretcher, Horne looked at Tree, seeing that his face was ashen, guessing his shock came not only from Goodair's blood-covered body but also from the realisation that he was now in command of the *Unity*. Or had the fact not yet occurred to the young man?

It was important to make Tree aware of his position. Horne turned to the surgeon. "Captain Goodair should be taken to his quarters unless—" he looked at Tree, "—unless Mr. Tree has different orders."

"Me?" Tree's eyes widened.

Horne turned back to the ruddy-faced surgeon. "I understand the ship's First Mate is suffering from a serious illness, Mr. Shanks."

"Aye, sir. Mr. Ames is in no shape to walk, let alone take command of this ship."

Horne watched Tree, waiting for him to realise that,

after the First Mate, he was next in command.

Tree's forehead beaded with perspiration; he pressed his lips tightly together; taking a deep breath, he said shakily, "Mr. Shanks, take Captain Goodair below to his . . . quarters."

"Aye, aye, sir."

The situation was delicate. Horne guessed that Tree was not qualified to assume command of the merchantman in its present situation. Not many officers in the Maritime Service were equipped to deal with a ship in battle.

Tree waited until Shanks and his mate had eased the stretcher down the companionway towards the round-house, then asked, "Captain Horne, what can I do?"

Horne looked astern, seeing the frigate changing tack. The only thing in the *Unity*'s favour at the moment was that the frigate had not yet made her stays.

He began, "Mr. Tree, the enemy's obviously changing tack to give us another pounding."

Tree repeated, "What can I . . . *do?*"

"Tack, Mr. Tree. You know the procedure, I presume."

"Aye, aye, sir."

Horne raised one hand to Tree's shoulder. "And stop saying 'Aye, aye, sir,' Tree. You're in command. Not me. Remember that."

Tree's brown eyes were big, round, filled with apprehension. "Will you stay to help me . . . sir?"

Horne nodded. "Captain Goodair kindly allowed me on his quarterdeck. I'd be honoured to remain here, Mr. Tree."

Tree sighed with relief.

Mustafa sat beneath the teak overhang of the forecastle, feeling the deck reverberate from gun fire. He remembered Horne's orders that the Marines were to stay out of action's way aboard the Indiaman, that the *Unity* was manned by the Maritime Service, men who resented the presence of Bombay Marines aboard their ship. Near Mustafa beneath the forecastle crouched Babcock, Bapu, Groot, Kiro, Jingee and Jud. Their different coloured faces formed a line of anxiety and glumness.

Trying to control his nerves, Mustafa sat playing with a rope, pulling it tight between his large hirsute fists, letting it slacken, tightening it again with a snap.

The rope Mustafa held—played with nervously—was no ordinary length of hemp. It was a garrotte, *one* of Mustafa's garrottes. He had possessed many in his life, garrottes made from hemp, cotton, wire, leather, even silk.

He had strangled his brother in Alanya, his home on Turkey's southern coast, with a cowhide garrotte. Having run away to Izmir to join the Sultan's Navy, he had served on an Ottoman ship until he had strangled a fellow seaman with a rattan garrotte. Jumping ship, he had joined an East India Company merchant vessel.

Having used a tightly-woven cotton garrotte on a Greek sailor aboard the Company ship, he had been convicted and sent to Bombay Castle where Horne had found him in an underground prison. For the first time in his life, Mustafa had been praised for his expertise with a garrotte.

Horne had taught Mustafa to use other weapons: sabres, knives, flintlocks, his head. Life as a Bombay Marine proved to be a life of fighting.

So why didn't Horne let him fight now? In this sea battle?

Mustafa realised there were rules—Navy rules, Company rules. But why did the East India Company have different rules for men who served aboard merchant ships

and for men who served aboard the Marine ships? To
Mustafa, that did not make sense.

From what he had seen of the *Unity* and its Maritime
Service, he was glad to be a Bombay Marine. Men aboard
this ship only wanted to collect their pay and return home
to their families; they sat around like girls dreading a
fight. They were not born to fight, they were born to hide
inside houses like women.

A sharp elbow disturbed Mustafa's brooding.

It was Babcock. He and Groot had recovered from their
sickness. He asked, "What do you say, you ugly Turk?"

Babcock was always asking Mustafa to "say" something. He claimed that Mustafa did not talk enough and
that Groot talked too much. But why should a man talk?
Mustafa feared that he would say the wrong thing if he
talked too much and would be sent back to gaol. Not to
the prisons beneath Bombay Castle—Horne had arranged
a pardon for Mustafa's last crime, as he had arranged an
amnesty for all the Bombay Marines whom he had recruited from prison. But there were crimes which Mustafa
had committed before Bombay Castle—men he had murdered, necks he had garrotted—all the way back to his
brother.

Babcock asked, "Do you want to fight or not?"

"Fight?" Mustafa snapped the garrotte between his two
ham-sized fists.

Babcock slugged the Turk on the shoulder. "I mean join
the gun crew. You can't go out there and . . . choke the
bloody enemy to death, man!"

Mustafa nodded towards the quarterdeck. "What about
orders?"

"From Horne?" Babcock frowned. "Can Horne invite
us all nice and politely to help save this ship's tired arse?

Hell no! Horne's busy himself trying to save it!"

Mustafa considered what Babcock had said. It did make sense. Horne had given the order in peace time, before the enemy attacked. So maybe Babcock was right.

Looking at Babcock, Mustafa nodded. "I want to fight."

Babcock pulled Mustafa up to his feet. The other Marines were already disappearing through the smoke spreading like ground fog from the roaring cannons.

5

A Dawn Flag

The wind strengthened from the northeast as dawn began bleaching the sky. Adam Horne had been awake for twenty-four hours but, troubled that Captain Goodair's wounds had left an inept officer of the Maritime Service in command of the *Unity*, he knew this was no time to think about sleep.

Taking stock of the damage done to the *Unity* by the frigate's attempted broadside, he saw that the aft bulwark had been shattered but not destroyed; the cro'jack and spanker sails were ripped, but the mast and all spars had mercifully escaped damage; so far, too, no reports of a strike had come from the lower decks.

Glancing aloft, he saw the morning's hands silhouetted against the pewter-grey sky, men following Horne's orders—passed through Tree—to bring the merchantman around to the wind. Amongst the seamen scrambling, swinging high above him, Horne saw a familiar shape, a black giant with both legs clenched around the mizzen topgallant yard. It was Jud! And next to him was Groot, tugging on gaskets, looking as healthy, as hearty as Horne remembered him from the days of the *Eclipse*.

Checking to see if more of his Marines had joined morning watch, Horne held the spyglass to his eye and searched the rigging.

Seeing no familiar faces, he looked to the larboard guns and, yes, there were Bapu and Mustafa ramming shot and charges into the guns, and at the starboard battery worked Babcock and Kiro, while Jingee ran water buckets.

Pleased that Babcock and Groot had obviously recovered from their sickness and that each of his men was contributing muscle to chores, Horne felt his spirits lift. The next stage of battle might not be as grim as he had anticipated. The addition of seven men might not alter a ship's fighting power, but Horne felt better knowing that the Marines whom he had come to consider to be his only true friends were safe and near him. Thoughts entered his mind about their next assignment and the nature of the orders waiting at Madagascar, but he put them out of his mind. Had not he told himself: Why speculate?

With a lighter heart, he looked through the spyglass, studying the frigate making her stays, swinging onto the new tack on the southeast horizon. Against the blur of approaching dawn, he noted that the frigate was close-hauled in the rising wind, and beyond her lay the patti-mar—the kingfisher leaving the two eagles to do battle.

Inching the spyglass back to the frigate, he studied her neat tumblehome, wondering who was the captain of this fine ship. Did the man have any idea of the chaos he'd caused aboard the *Unity*? That he had wounded the Company commander?

What was the enemy's goal? To destroy the merchant ship or merely cripple her and take her as a prize? There were also, he knew, Muslim raiders from Africa who captured crews from European ships, selling them to Ottoman slaveports along the Indian Ocean.

As the frigate approached beyond the starboard bow, Tree paced the windward side of the quarterdeck, bouncing Goodair's speaking trumpet behind his back and glancing nervously at Horne for instructions.

Horne had explained to Tree that the attack should come in two stages, two closely placed broadsides. His instructions had been simple but firm: Do not fire until you can successfully place the first of the two crippling blows.

As the vessels drew closer, an eerie stillness overtook the *Unity*, broken only by creaking timbers, sails snapping in the growing wind, waves crashing against the prow.

The moment was now imminent. Horne looked at Tree out of the corner of his eye before turning his attention back to the frigate's prow drawing in line with the *Unity*'s foremast.

Horne suspected that the enemy was attempting a similar tactic and, hoping to gain the jump on them by a few vital seconds, he gave Tree a nod.

Tree, his shaking hand raising the trumpet, his voice quavering, ordered, "Prepare to fire . . ."

The *Unity*'s timing must be precise; a fraction of a second too soon or late could mean the difference between success and possible annihilation.

Horne growled, *"Now!"*

"FIRE!" bellowed Tree, his face pouring perspiration.

Thunder ripped the morning; smoke clouds rose, engulfing the deck, but before the wind cleared the smoke, Horne repeated, "Now!" Tree repeated his bellow and another boom enveloped the deck, followed by a denser, deeper, higher cloud of pungent gun smoke.

The rumble from the two leviathans' weapons was cut by the screech of timber, the cries of mutilated men, the ever-present churning of iron-black waves. It seemed an eternity to Horne before the two ships creaked past one another; he ignored the damage done to the *Unity*, looking instead to see if their own guns had made a mark on the enemy.

A large cavity gaped from the frigate's starboard bulwark. Horne swept the spyglass astern to study the extending damage and it was then that he caught sight of the ship's named painted on the stern—*Huma*.

Tree threw his arms around Horne, crying jubilantly, "We did it! We did it!"

Horne stepped back, correcting, "*You* did it, Mr. Tree."

Tree guffawed, "As you say, *capitan*! As you say! And what do I do next?"

Admiring the young man's honesty, Horne nevertheless tried to be tactful. Despite wanting to assist Tree, he had to remember that this was a Company ship, and that the Company had insurance from Lloyd's Coffee House. If it were ever discovered that a man outside the Maritime Service had commanded the *Unity*, Lloyd's could refuse to pay for any damage done to the ship or cargo. In turn, the Company could ban Horne forever from the Bombay Marine or any other Company capacity, perhaps even keep him from ever finding a position again at sea.

Calmly, Horne answered, "Mr. Tree, I should imagine that, in such circumstances, Captain Goodair would first inspect his ship for possible damage."

"Yes, sir. Of course, sir."

Horne surveyed the main deck with a quick sweep of

the eye. "Although damage doesn't appear to be too extensive, Mr. Tree."

Tree drove the fist of one hand into the palm of the other. "No, but, by Gad, did we give them a taste of our guns!"

"Which means, Mr. Tree, they will be coming back for a powerful revenge."

Both men looked astern, seeing the frigate preparing to tack. Watching her sails, Horne remembered how the ship had impressed him as some mighty bird of prey and, studying her sails, he had a sudden inspiration, an idea how he—Mr. Tree—could clip that eagle's mighty wings.

A taste of victory had boosted the crew's spirits. If any of the men aboard the *Unity* had resented the presence of Bombay Marines on a Company merchantman, all ill feelings had disintegrated like the wisps of gun smoke. In their enthusiasm, they cheered the ship's Second Mate, Simon Tree, shouting, "Hip, hip, hooray!" while Tree blushed and bowed his head, accepting acclamation from men who usually sniggered at him behind his back for being a fool and lubber.

As dawn blotted the eastern sky, the *Unity*'s hands busily obeyed Tree's orders for the next battle manoeuvre, a simple ruse which Horne had explained to Tree. They would fire to cripple the *Huma* by bombarding her masts and sails, figuratively clipping the eagle's strong wings.

The enemy would be returning for a devastating reprisal, Horne was certain of that. He guessed, too, that they would try their damnedest to make a success of a broadside. The *Huma* was swinging a wide sweep in her new tack, telling Horne she was taking full advantage of her sea room to lay full aim at the *Unity*, to pound her from all gun decks.

The morning's changing winds had restored the weather gauge to the *Huma*, giving her superiority over the *Unity* in wind as well as gun power. But the rising gusts left both ships with less time to prepare for their deciding encounter.

A breeze against his cheek, Horne looked amidship for his own men, seeing Bapu with his red headband tied securely around his ears. The Indian warrior looked more like a weathered British seaman than someone who had been living in a Bombay elephant shed little more than seventy-two hours ago. Near him stood Babcock, who had ignored the gunners' advice, leaving his big ears unprotected against the gun blast.

Mustafa and Kiro remained attached to the starboard battery, and Jingee still hurried on water brigade. Telling himself he had no need to concern himself with his men, Horne turned to concentrate instead on Tree, to ensure that the Second Mate passed correct orders at the correct moment.

The enemy—whoever commanded the *Huma*—grew closer, threateningly, beyond the *Unity*'s larboard beam. Horne dropped the spyglass to watch her with his naked eye, waiting for the ship's close-hauled sails to approach the foremast of the merchantman.

Aware only of the sound of sluicing water, he ordered calmly, "It is time to commence, Mr. Tree."

His first success had firmed Tree's grip on the speaking trumpet and given a resounding confidence to his voice:

"Prepare . . . *guns*!"

Horne, his eye on the *Huma*'s bow, knew the strike must come sooner this time than the last broadside. He hoped he was not acting prematurely as he murmured, "Now, Mr. Tree."

"FIRE!"

Guns exploded; the *Unity* trembled; but the quake came from more than gun recoil. The enemy had fired at the same moment, Horne realised, pounding a devastating broadside against the *Unity*.

As thick, dense smoke rose from the bulwark, Horne looked for a sign of their own success and, yes, the *Huma*'s main topsail had altered, its yard gone completely, and the foresail had disappeared, the yard swinging from the rigging.

Remembering that the gunners had not been ordered to fire at will, Horne knew that Tree had to give the next command quickly and loudly. He shouted, "Mr. Tree, repeat!"

"Fire!" bellowed Tree.

The second round roared louder than the first, belching grape across the waves, raising smoke and soot, causing the deck to rumble. But a louder crash came from the broadside the *Huma* struck against the merchantman.

Hearing screams and painful cries rise around him, Horne feared the worst, but the air was too thick with smoke to see any carnage.

The deck canted beneath Horne's feet; battle continued around him, the fury between the two ships casting a black cloud across the sky. His eyes watered from the pungent smoke, and he was still unable to gauge any damage done to either vessel.

Tree's voice cut through the tumult. "Horne! Can you hear me, Horne? They're surrendering! They're surrendering to us, Horne!"

Surrendering? Horne's first instinct was one of distrust. False surrender was an old pirate trick.

Flailing his hands through the smoke, Tree shouted, "Look, sir! See! It's a flag! A white flag!"

Better than a white flag, Horne saw men diving into the water from the *Huma*. Still suspicious, fearing the enemy might try to assemble a boarding party for hand-to-hand combat, he looked toward the frigate's officers' deck.

He was surprised to see two turbaned men waving a flag, a length of cloth as white as new dawn and—all around them—their crew diving from the ship, clawing to swim towards the pattimar.

It was true. The enemy was surrendering, not fleeing. Their crew was abandoning ship. Why? Had the *Huma* been damaged? Was she sinking? Or were the crew deserting their leader like many Oriental troops did in defeat? Was that why the ship was not hurriedly taking flight?

Whatever the reason, Horne decided the *Unity* should make the most of the situation.

"Mr. Tree," he suggested. "What do you think about sending a shot across the prow of that pattimar?"

Tree's smile beamed through the soot caking his face. "Yes-s-s-s, sir!"

Horne turned to leave the quarterdeck, so that Tree could claim victory over both ships in full triumphal glory. He stopped abruptly when he saw Babcock at the foot of the companion ladder, looking up at him. The American was holding a mutilated body in his arms.

Horne lowered his eyes from Babcock's sooty face to the bleeding body in his arms. Despite gaping wounds in the man's chest, he recognised him by the bandanna tied around his ears. It was Bapu.

Horne asked, "Is he . . . dead?"

"Not yet."

Babcock moved towards the companionway, Bapu in his arms.

The battle over, candles were relit aboard the *Unity*. Horne adjusted his eyes to the near darkness as he followed Babcock, carrying Bapu, into the wardroom dotted with candles and serving as a sick bay. The odour of camphor, rum and sulphur cut through the sickening reek of the battle's worst scourge—burnt flesh.

The ginger-haired surgeon, Ronald Shanks, came towards Babcock, carrying a pot of linseed oil and lime water in one hand, an anodyne for the burn victims. He motioned Babcock to lower Bapu onto a table.

A low hum of moans filled the wardroom, a pathetic chorus punctuated by piercing screams from men with broken arms, legs or ribs, and by the delirious cries of those victims who had been driven out of their minds by pain.

As Babcock eased Bapu down onto the table, Horne moved to raise the straps to fasten around Bapu's lower legs, still thankfully intact, to prepare him for immediate surgery.

Shanks looked at the scarlet wetness of Bapu's gaping chest and shook his head.

Horne tightened, ready to force the surgeon to tend Bapu.

He demanded, "What the hell's the matter with you, Shanks?"

Shanks, tired and strained, began, "Sir, I can see now

that your man is—" He glanced down at Bapu's smeared face.

Bapu's eyelids fluttered. He looked from the surgeon to Horne. In a voice no louder than a whisper, he gasped, "Captain . . . Horne . . ."

Horne lowered his ear to Bapu's mouth. "Yes, man? What is it?"

"Don't argue with . . . old . . . sawbones . . ."

"You keep calm. You'll pull through this."

"No . . ." Bapu swallowed the blood welling in his mouth. "Don't waste time on . . . me . . ."

Horne glanced at Babcock.

Bapu grasped Horne's wrist and whispered hoarsely, "There's only one thing I'm sorry about . . . Captain . . ."

"What's that, man?"

"I'll never know if it was . . . was worth it . . ."

"Worth what?" asked Horne, holding out his hand for Bapu to grip in his pain.

"My waiting for our new mission . . . I'll never know now what the new mission will . . . be . . ."

Bapu choked, coughed, clung tighter to Horne's arm and, the next moment, Horne felt the big Indian's hand go limp, fall lifelessly onto the table. Bapu was dead.

6

Port Diego-Suarez

The cliffs of Madagascar rose above a long white beach lapped by the Indian Ocean, a welcome sight for the *Unity* trailing her two prizes, the *Huma* and the rake-sailed pattimar. The vessels belonged to the Omani pirate, Hoodad al Sur, a long-standing predator of the trade of the East India Company. Hoodad himself had not been aboard either ship but his lieutenant, Junah, had been captured from the *Huma* and was being taken in custody to Madagascar.

Captain Goodair ventured from his cabin at the hail of landfall. It was his first visit to the quarterdeck in the eight days since receiving his injuries. His pain had abated and Mr. Shanks kept his wounds dressed and a splint tied to his right arm. Goodair's legs had not been broken but he used a stick in his slow progress from the roundhouse to the quarterdeck.

A blue awning had been stretched across the quarterdeck, and Goodair invited Adam Horne to sit with him in the shade to enjoy tea and sesame cakes. Goodair's First Mate, Charles Ames, had not yet recovered from his illness, so the Second Mate, Simon Tree, remained the ship's acting senior officer. Horne knew that Goodair was on the way to recovery when the wry old commander said with a twinkle in his eye, "Mr. Tree must be uniquely grateful for your companionship on this voyage, Captain Horne."

Horne did not want to debunk any victory Tree might be claiming over the pirate ship. But neither did he want to spread lies.

"I think you have a loyal man in Tree, sir." He stopped himself from saying that he also thought that Tree was uncouth, loud and, at the same time, was too familiar with superior officers to make an effective commander himself.

The breeze was warm but Goodair clutched a Kashmiri robe to his throat. "I'm sorry to be parting company with you in Port Diego-Suarez, Captain Horne. I'd enjoy more of your companionship myself. All the way back to England."

"Thank you, sir. But duty for me begins in Diego-Suarez."

"Your days aboard the *Unity* have hardly been restful, Captain."

Horne hoped he did not sound arch as he answered, "Every voyage has its surprises, sir."

"As do you, Captain Horne. As do you."

Dreading what Goodair might be planning to say Horne kept his eyes on the distant cliffs, verdant foliage darkening their crests.

"I have spent more than a few hours in your company, Captain Horne," Goodair went on, "yet I feel as if I don't know you at all."

Horne was frequently accused of being secretive, overly protective of his privacy, drawing a circle around himself

and refusing to let anyone through. Believing there was
no reason to unfold his innermost thoughts, ambitions,
fears and pleasures, he replied, "I also enjoyed my time
with you, sir. Thank you."

Goodair knew he had overstepped social boundaries.
He said in a brighter voice, "You may rest assured, Captain Horne, that I shall inform your father what a fine son
he has. A boon to his name."

Horne had completed the letter to his father but was
having misgivings about sending it with Goodair. The letter was brief and, Horne feared, gloomy. Bapu's death
had left him desolate, and the last rites had been a grim,
painful farewell. Horne had wrapped the corpse in a hammock, sewing it shut and weighting the corners with shot.
He had dropped it into the Arabian sea as Jingee read
Praise For A Rajput Warrior. After the brief ceremony,
Horne had tried to keep himself busy making repairs to
the *Unity* and working aboard the *Huma*. The pirate frigate was Bombay-built, finer than Horne's expectation.
Tree had asked him to take command of it for the re-
mainder of the voyage to Port Diego-Suarez, but Horne
had adamantly refused, explaining that the East India
Company would probably judge both the frigate and pattimar to be war prizes for the Maritime Service, distrib-
uting the reward money among the officers and crew. It
would therefore be highly improper for an officer of the
Bombay Marine to bring the *Huma* into port; there was
already enough hostility between the Maritime Service
and Bombay Marine.

Tree, joining Horne and Goodair under the canopy on
the quarterdeck, made his farewell to Horne, concluding,
"Captain Horne, sir, you've taught me to respect the—"
he raised his voice—"Bombay . . . *Buccaneers*!"

Horne flinched. Tree had obviously meant no offence but he explained, "Mr. Tree, a Marine goes into battle when someone calls him a 'buccaneer.' "

Bewildered, Tree looked from Horne to Goodair. "But ... but ... but ... I've always heard Bombay Marines called 'buccaneers'!"

"Slang, dear boy, slang," interrupted Goodair, clutching the robe to his neck. "An unflattering description of the Company's brave Marine."

Tree lowered his head. "I'm sorry, sir. I had no idea, sir."

Horne realised there were many things which Simon Tree did not know. He doubted, however, if any of those short-comings, major or trivial, would prevent the young man from rising in the Honourable East India Company's Maritime Service.

Madagascar, the shoe-shaped island off Africa's southeast coast, was separated from the mainland by the two-hundred-and-fifty-mile wide Strait of Mozambique. The first Europeans to visit Madagascar had been the Portuguese in the sixteenth century. In the following two hundred years, the island had been controlled by a succession of English, French and local Malagasy rulers. At present, the English were temporarily back in command of Madagascar, the fourth largest island in the world.

Fred Babcock learned these facts in an open boat while crossing from the *Huma* to the stone quay of Port Diego-Suarez. Horne had given his men the morning to explore the small settlement located at the island's northern tip and Babcock, knowing that Horne was paying an official visit to Company House, guessed that the call concerned their new assignment which their Captain would later explain to his men.

Two wine shops flanked the small harbour and, by late morning, men off the *Unity* had settled under the shady bamboo awnings or had drifted off into the surrounding streets, exploring the white-washed settlement for other public establishments. Groot, Kiro, Jud and Mustafa were grouped around Jingee and an old Malagasy villager, a shrivelled little man whom Jingee was questioning in Bantu about the island's people, asking why they looked Oriental rather than African.

At the moment Babcock was more interested in food than in local people or their ways; he decided to search out a cook shop.

In the past, Babcock had been suspicious of native food, but he was convinced now that it was Groot's cooking that had made him sea-sick. Groot had prepared a Dutch hot-pot on the day when the press gang had surprised them and Mustafa, who had refused to eat Groot's stew, had not fallen ill. Babcock decided it would be safer eating local dishes than anything the Dutch Marine concocted. As he left the main square, he was dreaming of a bowl of rice, some thick sauces, fresh pastries stuffed with lamb, cheese, dates, nuts, or a combination of some of them, if not all.

The day was hot, but a sea breeze cooled the hillside. Babcock walked between the rows of low houses topped with thatched roofs, emerging into a small opening—more of a triangle than a square. A cluster of familiar faces from the *Unity* had gathered in front of a clay building, each man holding a large bamboo cup.

"Babcock, my boyo! Come and join us!" shouted the gunner's mate.

A red-haired man held up his cup. "Try the local poison, Cockers!"

A bewhiskered Scotsman invited, "Aye, take a swill with us, laddie."

The *Unity* must wait here at Port Diego-Suarez for the merchant convoy to arrive from the China Sea. Babcock knew that seamen often became restless in port, drinking too much, usually ending up quarrelling or worse. Knowing he was likely to find himself in the middle of a fistfight, he decided to keep trudging up the hill.

Company House sat on the crest, a sprawling white building which commanded a sweeping view over the deep-water harbour and the turquoise sea beyond. As Babcock passed the ornately wrought gates guarding the drive, he thought of Horne who was inside the large house at that very moment, probably receiving orders which could affect the next few months, possibly even years.

Thinking about Horne, Babcock remembered how upset he had been by Bapu's death. Babcock did not know much about the Indian caste system, only that there were four main castes, and that Bapu had supposedly been born into one of the highest, the caste of warriors. But Babcock thought that Bapu had been very like himself, a man who did not follow the life set out for him. Instead of being a valiant warrior serving some maharajah or even the Grand Moghul, Bapu had been a thief, the leader of a mountain band which had attacked Company supply wagons in Rajasthan.

Babcock himself should have been a farmer. Back in Ohio, he would almost have been gentry by now—upright, respectable, a husband and father, probably even an elder in the church. But Babcock had quarrelled with his father and run away to sea. Aboard a ship out of Boston, an officer had goaded him about his hulking size; he was forever pushing Babcock, finally forcing him into a fight. Babcock had defended himself but, unfortunately, the officer had struck his head on a capstan and died, and Babcock had been imprisoned in Bombay Castle.

When Horne had chosen his men from the underground prisons at Bombay Castle, Babcock had suspected he was taking them to another prison, or to form some kind of work gang. They had gone to a penal colony, certainly, but Horne had taken them there—to Bull Island—only to separate the wheat from the chaff, to school his recruits to be a squadron of highly-trained saboteurs.

During the few short weeks that Babcock had spent with Horne on Bull Island and, later, at Madras, he had felt as if he were being set back on the right path in life; Horne believed in him, and in his abilities. Babcock suspected, too, that the other men respected Horne as much as he did, and were as grateful to him.

As for the new mission, what would it be like? Would it last longer than the foray into Fort St. George at Madras? Would they remain together afterwards like a true unit? Babcock and Horne's other men were Bombay Marines, yes, but they avoided conscription aboard Marine ships, voyages that would take them on chart-making expeditions, locking them into a life of drudgery.

A chattering sound disturbed Babcock's reflections.

To the left of the stone path he saw a pile of bamboo cages containing monkeys; the animals were gripping the bamboo slats, baring their brown teeth at Babcock as an old crone in front of the cages held out a hand to him, asking, "Buy? Buy? Buy?"

7

Company House

Adam Horne's first clue to the identity of the man who would be receiving him at Company House came when a secretary said that His Excellency, Governor Spencer, was not expecting Horne to arrive in Madagascar until the following week.

Governor Spencer of Bombay, a slim man with a meticulously trimmed moustache and pointed goatee, was wearing a neatly cut but unfashionable frock-coat when he greeted Horne in a second-storey room in Company House. After a curt handshake, he nodded to a pair of gilt chairs in front of the tall, shuttered windows, saying, "Let us sit there."

Horne sat down, his back to the window, cocked hat on his knee. He had met Spencer on only two previous occasions, both brief, before he had captured General Lally from Madras, a mission which had been ordered by Spencer and his two fellow Governors, Pigot of Madras and Vansittart of Bengal.

Dispensing with any social niceties, Spencer came

straight to the point. "As you're well aware, Captain Horne, the war with France is entering its sixth year."

Horne kept his eyes on Spencer's gaunt face, his complexion apparently untouched by India's harsh weather which turned most men's skin to leather.

The Governor, his voice clipped and impatient, went on. "The two countries seem to have reached a stalemate. The fighting has come to a lull. In the meantime, the French are still plagued with the problem which led to Lally's downfall at Pondicherry: lack of money."

Commodore Watson had also mentioned money, Horne remembered. Had Watson known that Spencer was waiting to see him in Port Diego-Suarez? If so, why had he not said anything about it?

Spencer continued, "But only in the past weeks, Captain Horne, have we heard about a consignment of gold being shipped from France to pay their troops in Mauritius."

Commodore Watson *had* known about the mission, Horne was sure of it, but the Governors had obviously forbidden him to say anything about it. So the old walrus had done his best by uttering hints about a treasure ship.

"The British Navy Board has instructed the East India Company to intercept the French gold shipment, Captain Horne. That's why we are turning to you."

Without waiting for Horne's response, Spencer rose from his chair and moved to a large, delicately painted map stretched on the wall.

Pointing to the pastel-green tip of Africa, he said, "Governor Pigot, Governor Vansittart and myself are calling upon you, Captain Horne, to commandeer the French war chest between the Cape of Good Hope and—"

As Spencer pointed to a small dot directly east of Madagascar—Mauritius—Horne noticed that the Governor's fingernails were torn and ragged. Apart from being at variance with his neat appearance, the bitten nails betrayed that he was a very troubled man.

"With all due respect, Your Excellency, why does the Navy Board not dispatch its own ships on this mission?"

Horne's question surprised Spencer. Looking over his shoulder, he studied the man sitting in the chair, his grey eyes dulling as he formed his answer.

Turning from the map, he nodded, explaining, "His Majesty's Navy are servants of the King, Captain Horne. When England signs a peace treaty with France—an event which we see as being imminent—England will be made to repay any gold taken in war."

"Does not the Company's charter give it the same responsibility as the state, Your Excellency? Would not gold taken from a French ship by the Honourable East India Company also have to be returned by articles of an international treaty?"

Spencer's face softened. "Yes. But only if the East India Company could be directly connected with the . . . event—which it will not be if the attack goes as we hope it will."

Horne began to understand. "The Navy Board—as well as the Company—want unidentifiable raiders to seize the French war chest."

"In a manner of speaking, yes."

"That's why you're turning to—" Horne decided that only the Marines' loathsome nickname would be appropriate, "—the Bombay buccaneers."

"Precisely."

"But why choose *me* to lead the mission, Your Excellency?"

"Your performance at Madras makes you the most likely candidate, Captain Horne."

"I had the *Eclipse*."

Spencer turned away from Horne. "I understand, Captain, that your recent voyage from Bombay to Madagascar was itself interrupted by raiders. I also understand that you helped thwart the attack as well as capture two ships, one of which is a frigate, a fine, strong ship called the *Huma*."

Who told him that? Goodair? Tree?

Spencer continued, "Even as we talk, Captain Horne, below us in the harbour the *Huma* is undergoing repairs—masts replaced, guns fitted, entirely provisioned and crewed."

Horne refused to allow himself to become excited about the possibility of the majestic *Huma* being assigned to his command. Instead, his voice sharpened as he asked, "What ship would have been assigned for the mission had the *Huma* not been captured, Your Excellency?"

The young man's questions disturbed Governor Spencer. He did not like subordinates being so thorough.

He replied, "A Company brig was to have been spared."

"How, sir, can one ship—brig *or* frigate—hope to take an entire convoy?"

"You're assuming that the French gold is travelling in convoy, Captain Horne. Our sources in France report that the gold departed six months ago from Le Havre aboard a ship called the *Royaume*."

"And the ship is still at sea, sir?"

"Yes."

"With all due respect, sir, how do you receive information so quickly?"

"The *Royaume* is also laden with cargo, Captain. Heavy cargo. Progress is slow."

Horne thought of one possibility of danger. "Could not Mauritius also have been alerted and be sending an escort for the *Royaume* when she passes into the Indian Ocean?"

"That could be dealt with."

"Am I to understand by that remark, Your Excellency, that Pocock's fleet will also be participating in the operation? If only in a minor capacity?"

"Admiral Pocock and His Majesty's Navy will be kept informed, yes."

It was on the tip of Horne's tongue to argue that word passed by sea messenger would not help him and his men in a difficult situation, not if they needed immediate support.

Spencer said, "You look troubled, Captain Horne. Why? At Madras, the odds against success were much greater."

"At Madras, Your Excellency, you and your distinguished colleagues supplied me with ground plans for Fort St. George. Watch charts. Time lists. I have nothing now except a fairly dated report saying that the French have dispatched a treasure chest—aboard a ship named the *Royaume*—destined for the island of Mauritius." Unimpressed, Horne shrugged.

"Ah, but you do have a squadron of highly trained Marines, Captain Horne. Six of them."

Not seven? Governor Spencer's source of information about the Marines must be impeccable, including the news of Bapu's death. Horne had an inexplicable feeling that his enemy might easily be not the French, but England's Honourable East India Company.

•   •   •

Horne had left Company House. Governor Spencer sat at a table in a small room, holding the letter which Horne had written to his father in London. Chips from the wax seal were scattered across the table's leather top.

Reading the simply-written communication, Spencer liked Horne even less than he did in person. The letter's tone was like Horne himself: straightforward, yes, but it seemed to be hiding something. As Horne did.

Horne had written of a leader's responsibility to his troops, of man's need to be constantly ready for death, of the fact that death in a distant, alien land was not as terrifying as the prospect of death in one's homeland.

Reading these thoughts, Spencer wondered what kind of relationship a son had with his father when he could write to him about such ideas instead of gossiping about cousins and marriages and blisters, and too much rice and not enough potatoes. Spencer pictured the red-nosed tradesman who had sired him and felt a strange, new jealousy of Horne.

Despite the fact that it was no normal letter home, the pages contained no mention of any mission, no facts which Horne might have deduced from Watson and was passing on to his father. The Honourable East India Company was insisting that there must be no hint to anyone— not even family, especially an influential family like Horne's—about the assignment to seize the French war chest. Ramifications were going to be difficult enough without unnecessary inquiries. The undertaking was volatile.

Putting aside the letter, Spencer rang a silver bell on the table to summon his secretary. The letter could be resealed and given back to Goodair to deliver in London. Spencer also made a mental note that Goodair must somehow be rewarded by the Company for his co-operation in handing over the letter. Perhaps a ceremonial sword, something given to him at a Company banquet, something to make the old man swell his pigeon chest.

As he sat waiting, Spencer decided that what troubled him most about Adam Horne was his lack of resemblance to most young men who came out to India. In general they were running away from gambling debts in England; from a wife, from scandal or crime. Although rumour had it that Horne had fled London after his fiancée had been murdered by a well-bred-hooligan, Spencer had the distinct feeling that he had come to India not running from anything, but looking for something. But what? Who? Why?

Horne troubled Spencer. He was a puzzle, an aristocrat by attitude if not birth, who lived by his own rules. Spencer's one consolation was that young men like Adam Horne did not know what a relentless world they lived in, that they were innocent creatures compared to men like Spencer who had to plot, connive, juggle right and wrong to reach a profitable end. Men like Spencer used men like Adam Horne.

8

Monkey-face

Adam Horne strolled down the hill from Company House wishing there was some way to be a Bombay Marine without being connected to the East India Company. Involvement with them made him feel dishonest. He too often suspected them of dishonourable activities, sensing that his work helped unlikeable men to achieve ignoble ends.

Horne held no illwill against commerce. His father was a banker, and the profits from business had fed and clothed him since childhood. But the size of the East India Company was now giving businessmen the power of kings, allowing them control over life and death. To Horne's mind, this privilege was exceedingly dangerous.

In 1600 Queen Elizabeth had granted a royal charter to a collection of English merchants who wanted to participate in the wealth being brought back to Europe from the Orient by Dutch and Portuguese trading companies. Quickly surpassing Holland and Portugal, England had also overtaken France's East India Company, the *Com-*

pagnie des Indes Orientales, turning a war with France from a struggle for trade into a battle for territory.

One hundred and sixty-one years after its conception, England's East India Company possessed more wealth, more power than most nations. In recent years Horne had seen how the Governors were beginning to increase the Company's profits with the help of the sword, deposing Indian rulers who refused to grant them trading rights, planting company puppets on native thrones. Robert Clive, the former Governor of Bengal, had been the first man to hold a Company post as well as a commission in the Army. Retiring to London on his vast wealth from India, Clive was considered to be the richest man in the world.

Suspicious of Governor Spencer's real reasons—together with those of his two colleagues, Pigot of Madras and Vansittart of Bengal—for sending the Company's Marines to seize the French war chest, Horne reached the bottom of the hill, wondering if the Governors were trying to fuel a mutiny within the French forces. A mutiny could rid the East Indies of the French once and for all.

Or did the British Navy Board truly want the French war chest for their own coffers, needing the gold to finance other colonial campaigns in, say, Canada? Despite his pleasure at being given the *Huma*, Horne suspected that there was some sinister motive behind this sea venture.

The sounds of a bare-knuckle fight made him pause at an opening between the sun-bleached houses and, looking through the gap, he saw a group of men shouting and laughing.

.   .   .

More than thirty men had formed a tight circle around the combatants and were calling out encouragement:

"Give him a taste of your knuckles, Dave!"

"Smash that monkey-face!"

"Show the Bombay buccaneer who's a man!"

The mention of "Bombay buccaneer" alerted Horne. Pushing his way through the circle, he saw the heads of two men, recognising one of them as Babcock, the other as Dave Linderman, the boatswain's mate from the *Unity*, a bear of a man with a pug-nose and bushy side-whiskers.

"Hit him harder, Dave!"

"Bloody that American blow-hard!"

"Black and blue the big lubber!"

Babcock was fast on his feet for a man of his size; he was dancing around Linderman, throwing alternating blows of his fists in quick, hard-hitting succession—the left, the left, the right—knuckles cracking against Linderman's face, breaking his skin, smashing his nose, pummelling his ears.

Bobbing to the left and right, Linderman had failed to avoid most of Babcock's punches; blood was streaming from his nose, and his lower lip was cut and swollen. The crew, however, continued to cheer Linderman and jeer at Babcock.

Linderman struck a blow to Babcock's ribs and repeated the strike, concentrating on this target with a burst of new energy. Doubling over, Babcock brought his elbows to his side as the cheers rose for Linderman.

Bursting from the crouch, Babcock wrapped his left arm around Linderman's neck, locking the seaman's head under his upper arm like a wrestler, and began driving his fist against Linderman's face.

Horne saw that Babcock might seriously injure his opponent if he continued. Bolting forward, he grabbed Babcock by the shoulder, separating the two men.

Babcock spun, ready to attack his new opponent, but seeing it was Horne, he hesitated, gasping, "What the hell—?"

Horne moved between him and Linderman. "Get out of here, Babcock."

"Hell I will! They started it!"

Horne wanted to collect his Marines and tell them the news about the *Huma*, perhaps help join the work being done on the frigate.

As the seamen backed away, subdued by the sight of the gold-trimmed uniform, Horne repeated, "Babcock, get out of here."

A man called from the circle, "Go on, you big monkey! Go with him!"

Babcock pointed at the man. "Hear that? Hear what they called me? Monkey!"

"Monkey!" shouted another seaman. "You look just like your kid!"

Babcock lunged for the man.

Grabbing Babcock by the shoulder, Horne raised a fist to his face. At the same moment, a small, nut-brown monkey wrapped its small furry arms around Horne's leg and leaped, chattering, to swing from Horne's bicep to Babcock's shoulder, hugging Babcock's neck and licking his blood-streaked face with a wide, wet tongue.

Horne demanded, "Whose is that?"

Babcock wiped perspiration mixed with blood from his brow. "Mine."

PART TWO
"Pass the Parcel"

9

The *Huma*

Horne awoke to the absence of gulls mewing, the first time in five days that the scavenger birds had not awakened him with their tormenting chorus. Having cleared Madagascar, the *Huma* had emerged from the southern waters of the Strait of Mozambique and had passed far enough east from Africa to be rid of the foul, harping land birds.

Leaping from his berth, he grabbed the twill trousers he had substituted for the breeches of his uniform. Three sharp knocks sounded on the cabin door as he stood looking to see where he had tossed the *dungri* shirt he had sleepily pulled off last night after studying charts, examining current flows, estimating where—and when—the *Huma* might spot the French treasure ship.

Calling for the early morning visitor to enter the cabin, Horne was not surprised to see Jingee carrying in a breakfast tray. He never ceased to be amazed by the way the young Tamil found time to perform watch duties as well as act as his valet, personal cook and *dubash*. Horne had eaten better since leaving Port Diego-Suarez six days ago than he had in six months in Bombay.

The distribution of duty aboard the *Huma* was prejudiced, Horne knew. He had appointed his Marines to positions of officer rank aboard the frigate. Whilst he was familiar with the abilities of his men, he knew nothing about the recruits whom the East India Company had gathered on Madagascar. Governor Spencer had culled a skeleton crew from three Company ships in harbour and from the sailors who had previously served aboard the *Huma*. He had also found a handful of young islanders anxious to escape the tedium of their villages. The result was a shipful of lascars, pirates, fishermen—a motley crew over whom Horne's six Marines had command.

Jingee, proud to be one of the *Huma*'s new "officers," still wore his turban, *dhoti* and loose cotton shirt. Transferring a plate and bowl from the bamboo tray to Horne's desk, he announced, "The wind's strong from the west this morning, Captain sahib."

"Hmmm." Horne stood on one foot, pulling on a tall leather boot, the footgear being the only part of his uniform he chose to wear aboard the frigate.

Jingee continued arranging Horne's breakfast on the desk rather than setting a proper table. The bowl of fruit he placed on the neatly pressed cloth was more for ornamentation than consumption. Horne suspected that if he asked for a vaseful of flowers to decorate his table, Jingee would somehow produce roses or lilies or field flowers in the middle of the Indian Ocean.

Ramming his foot into the second boot, Horne inhaled the tempting aroma wafting from the steaming dishes. He normally did not enjoy eating in the morning, but Jingee inevitably prepared some tempting fare—hot bread laced with cinnamon, porridge dotted with succulent raisins, fruit-flavoured teas.

Curious about the activity on the quarterdeck, Horne reconfirmed as he moved to the desk, "Jud's morning watch?"

"Yes, Captain sahib. And Groot's sailing master at the wheel." Jingee turned to a locker, took out a freshly laundered shirt and passed it to Horne, holding out his hand for the wrinkled garment that Horne had picked up from the arm of the chair.

Surrendering the soiled shirt, Horne asked, "What about the new men?"

Jingee tossed the shirt towards the door where he would not miss it on the way out of the cabin. Crossing to the berth to straighten Horne's bed linen, he answered, "The new men ask questions all the time about Marines, Captain sahib. They don't understand the ways of Bombay Marines."

Who did understand the Bombay Marines? Particularly those in Horne's squadron? Manning a pirate frigate and searching for a French treasure ship—Horne's Bombay Marines must seem normal to very few outsiders.

"The new hands," continued Jingee, "think that a Marine should be—" he nodded at the door, "—a guard. A sentinel. A man who stands in the companionway with a musket on his shoulder." Jingee stood rigidly, chest thrown out, both arms at his sides to illustrate his point.

"That's how a Marine should be, Jingee. Aboard other ships. Navy ships."

Jingee bent over the wrinkled bed linen. "But not the *Huma*."

"Nor the *Eclipse*. Nor any ship over which I have had command, and probably will ever have command."

Horne preferred a crew to be versatile, capable of as many feats as possible; he also believed that the men themselves preferred their duty to be that way.

"Do you know what the name means, Captain sahib?"

"What name, Jingee?"

"The *Huma*?"

Horne had never thought about it. "No. What?"

"It's a mythical bird. A bird in Indian folklore which never stops flying."

"A bird that's always in flight?" Horne thought of the noisy seagulls which had thankfully disappeared from the stern windows.

"The *Huma* flies day and night, Captain sahib. Never alights on a tree or a rock or a fence. Always staying in air."

Horne was intrigued. He remembered how he had first visualised the frigate when he had seen it from the Indiaman, seeing it as a large, magnificent eagle, travelling with a smaller predator, a kingfisher.

Bending over the berth, Jingee smoothed the sheet, saying, "That's a sad story, don't you think, Captain sahib? A bird that can never stop flying?"

"Perhaps for a nesting bird, yes. But not for a predator, a hunter, or for a messenger. The gift of staying in motion could be a great attribute, Jingee. A wonderful gift. A fine feat."

Jingee stood upright, surprised by Horne's opinion.

"Imagine it," Horne went on. "Such a bird would not have to waste time resting, taking food, sleeping. It would always have the strength to keep on flying, discovering new things, travelling to new places, encountering new things."

Jingee bent back over the berth, shaking his head; he

decided that Horne, the Captain sahib, would probably be such a bird rather than a nice, cosy nesting bird, a partridge or a dove.

Horne picked some raisins from the porridge, eating them like sweets. "Do you think the name's an omen, Jingee?" he asked.

"Omen, Captain sahib?"

"For us? That we'll always be on the wing? Never remaining in one place?"

"I shall ask the astrologer, Captain sahib, when we return to Bombay."

"And if we don't drop anchor, you'll have your answer."

Jingee laughed at Horne's flippant remark. Moving towards the door, he glanced at him with admiration, knowing why he respected him. A stern, dedicated man, Horne also had a whimsical side to him, an appreciation of the mysterious, the unknown, the sacred. Jingee truly believed that Horne possessed great *karma*, that intangible, indefinable essence of a man's soul.

Seated behind his desk, Horne spooned his porridge as he studied a chart for Cape Agulhas. "Jingee," he asked, "have there been complaints from the crew about their food?"

Jingee cooked for Horne and, occasionally, for the other Marines, but never for the crew. The ship's galley had a Malagasy cook. But Jingee had seen their provisions and answered, "The food is bad, Captain sahib. There are weevils in the biscuits. The dried fish is too salty. The barrel meat is tough as leather."

Horne had feared this. He had seen one cask of salt fish after weighing anchor and had turned up his nose at the stench. At Port Diego-Suarez, he had been too busy supervising the ship's refitting to attend to its provisioning. His first instincts on discovering the inferior condition of the supplies at sea had been to share his own food with the crew, but Jingee had pointed out that there would not even be enough staples from Horne's provisions for one complete galley meal.

Why had Governor Spencer done such a thing? Horne wondered. Or had some local merchant taken advantage of the Company's situation and produced old rations, a sad but familiar trick?

Jingee frowned. "If anybody gets hungry, I know where they can get a fat monkey to cook."

Horne raised his eyes. He knew what monkey Jingee meant.

Jingee gripped an imaginary knife, threatening, "I'm going to kill that monkey myself, Captain sahib."

Fred Babcock had kept the nut-brown monkey from Madagascar and brought it aboard the *Huma*, arguing that Navy ships had dogs and cats, so why could not the Bombay Marine have a monkey?

Jingee shook his head, saying, "You'll see, Captain sahib. You'll see. Babcock will bring that monkey to this morning's meeting. You'll see how loudly it chatters and screams."

A meeting had been slotted between the morning and the late morning watch. Horne hoped no altercation would develop between his men because of a monkey; he had too many important details to discuss.

Babcock's pet monkey added to Jingee's disapproval of the towering American Marine. A man who did not properly address his superiors was not a man to be admired. Jingee had always secretly disapproved of Babcock's disrespectful ways but, of course, had tried hard not to betray any of his feelings. He had noticed, however, that Babcock seldom saluted Horne, that he seldom addressed him as "sir" or "sahib" or "*schipper*," or however people addressed officers in that far-off land across the Pacific Ocean called the Americas.

Jingee thought about Fred Babcock—and his annoying little brown pet monkey—as he washed Horne's laundry. Using ash soap that he carried tied around his waist in a leather pouch, he crouched in the space which seamen used for their latrine, the enclosure at the fore part of the ship and named for its location—the "heads."

Rubbing a shirt's collar, his thoughts moved to another Marine, Bapu. What was happening to Bapu? How would he come back to earth in the divine cycle of existence? Would he return to relive his role as a warrior? Or would Bapu's forebears consider that he had forsaken the *Kshatriya* caste? Being disowned, Bapu would be reborn outside the system of the four castes, coming back a *Panchama*—somebody so deplorable that people would not touch him. Perhaps he would even be reincarnated as someone who had to ring a bell to warn unsuspecting strangers that his polluting presence was approaching them.

Not wanting to wash Horne's clothing in harsh, salty sea water, Jingee rinsed the shirt in a bucket of drinking water he had taken unnoticed from the casks. As he worked, he thought about the rest of the Marines. He had definite opinions about each and every one of them.

Mustafa and Groot had been good friends of Babcock in Bombay; the three of them had lived together. But, then, they were *topiwallahs*—foreigners who wore hats, not turbans. In fact, Groot never took off that blue cap.

Did he wear it for some religious reason? Was he some kind of northern Sikh?

Thinking of religion, Jingee reflected that Mustafa was a Muslim. Muslim invaders had come to India more than three hundred years ago and put their Grand Moghul on the throne. The Hindu Tamils in the south had never accepted the Moghul's religion, but many northern Indians not only bowed to the mighty court of wealth and power but accepted the word of Allah.

Jud—also a Muslim—mystified Jingee more than Mustafa. To Jingee, Mustafa was little better than a thug. A tough. But, Jud, ah, he was different. He was special.

Jingee considered that Jud must be an exceptional man for the priests of the Red Temple to allow him to guard their fabulous treasures. Hindu priests were *Brahmins*, the highest caste in all creation, and if *Brahmins* recognised something unique in Jud, then he must be no common thief. He must have great *Karma*. Jingee often heard Jud singing to the wind and suspected it was some kind of religious chant, some conversation with spirits.

The Japanese Marine, Kiro, frightened more than baffled Jingee. Japanese Orientals and Asian Orientals were similar, yet so different. All Bombay Marines were supposed to be accomplished assassins. Jingee had killed his previous employer—an English district officer—who had defied Hindu law by yoking a Brahmin to an Untouchable to till his kitchen garden. Jingee had warned the foreigner that he was violating sacred laws. But the foreigner had continued to ignore Jingee's warning and Jingee had driven a dagger through the man's sacrilegious heart. For that crime Jingee had been condemned to Bombay Castle.

Kiro, however, was a different kind of murderer. He was stealthy, quiet, his eyes like water at night. Seldom talking, never divulging secrets. Yes, Jingee had to admit to himself that if he were to fear any of the Bombay Marines, it would be Kiro.

He stood wringing water from Horne's laundry over the blue-grey waves lapping below, thinking of the way the Captain sahib held together this unusual assortment of men. Without Horne, the Marines would not talk to each other, not see each other, not even know each other. They were united by Horne and, of course, by their criminal backgrounds. But the important link was the Captain sahib.

Pulling out a length of string from the side of his *dhoti*, Jingee knotted it across the heads, letting the wind off the sea begin drying the wet laundry. The morning was hot. The clothes would dry quickly. Jingee was not on watch duty, so he could stand here waiting until it was time for the morning meeting. If somebody wanted to use the heads, Jingee did not care. They could go somewhere else. His work came first. The Captain sahib reigned supreme.

The six Marines came to Horne's cabin for the meeting. Seeing them gathered so casually inside the small space reminded Horne of the old days aboard the *Eclipse*.

Pressing on with business at hand, he addressed them standing at his desk. "I haven't informed you about the purpose of our new assignment for the simple reason that we've had more important things to occupy our minds. But now that the *Huma*'s at sea, I can tell you the bad news—we've been deputed to find a needle in a haystack."

Glancing from Babcock with his monkey by the door, to Mustafa cross-legged on the deck, to the other four men lounging or squatting around the cabin, he continued,

"We're here to find a French ship, the *Royaume*. She sailed from Le Havre six months ago carrying a shipment of gold. She's bound for Mauritius. Our orders are to commandeer her."

Babcock whistled.

"Apart from the gold," elaborated Horne, "the *Royaume* is supposedly carrying heavy cargo. Disguising her true mission, I suppose. Whatever the reason, the cargo's in our favour as it slows down her progress."

Groot, sitting cross-legged to Horne's right, raised his hand.

Horne nodded permission to speak.

"*Schipper,*" he began, using the Dutch word for captain. "How is the French ship armed?"

"We don't know, Groot. Incidentally, how do our guns stand?" He looked at Kiro.

Kiro had been a gunner aboard a Japanese pirate boat out of Nagasaki, learning English from a Lascar sailor before being captured in an attack on an East India Company merchantman and jailed in Bombay Castle. Because of his experience Horne had appointed him gunner aboard the *Huma*.

Sitting on deck in front of Horne's berth, Kiro answered, "Larboard guns are stronger than starboard, sir."

Horne said, "We must try for perfect balance, Kiro. Also, I want swivel guns ready on the forecastle."

"Aye, aye, sir."

Horne's hazel eyes moved from Kiro to Jud squatting next to him, and then to Jingee, the only Marine able to stand up straight without brushing his head on the cabin's low beams.

"If any of you men have questions, ask them. We can always work out some kind of plan. The orders are difficult but not impossible. We've had a tougher command."

Babcock laughed. "That's the trouble. We shouldn't have done so well."

"Are you afraid, Babcock?"

Babcock answered honestly, one hand stroking the monkey cradled on his arm. "Not of having to find a needle in a haystack. But set against a treasure ship better armed than us, hell, yes, I'm . . . afraid!"

"We know nothing of its munitions," Horne reminded Babcock.

Jud asked, "What about her escort, sir?"

"My information, Jud, is that the *Royaume* left Le Havre unescorted."

Horne resettled himself on the edge of the desk. "But I'll say this. If there *is* an escort, if the *Royaume is* sailing in convoy, we shall abandon the mission. Immediately. No permission asked."

Jud smiled. "Sir, you of all men would find a way to sneak us into a convoy and make away with a gold chest."

Horne glowed, not above enjoying idle flattery.

Groot called, "What we are doing now, *schipper*, is patrolling all southern waters for a French ship."

"Yes, Groot. In effect. The winds fortunately narrow down the work for us. After rounding the Cape of Good Hope to Cape Agulhas, the Roaring Forties should bring the *Royaume* directly into our path."

Jingee asked, "Is it possible, Captain sahib, that the French ship has already passed?"

"Or pirates got to the gold before us?" put in Jud.

"Those are both possibilities," said Horne. "We merely have to continue our search, looking, waiting, hoping."

He glanced around the cabin. "Any more questions?"

There was a silence broken only by the sound of the

Huma sailing under full canvas, the creak of timbers, the prow cutting through lapping waves.

Horne looked at Mustafa, realising that the Turk had been silent throughout the entire morning's meeting.

"Mustafa, do you have any questions?"

The beefy Turk began to speak but stopped, shaking his head, his thick black moustache turning down at both bushy ends.

"What is it, Mustafa? Something's troubling you?"

Glancing around the cabin with quick, darting eyes, Mustafa looked back at Horne and asked, "What do we do with the gold, sir, when we get it?"

Laughter filled the cabin.

Horne raised both hands for silence. "Return it to Bombay—"

Mustafa's face fell.

Horne's answer had only been a quick response, and he added, "You didn't think we were going to be able to keep it, did you, Mustafa?"

"Sir, if there's a lot of it and we're the only ones who know where it is—"

The men laughed louder.

Horne smiled, realising, however, that Mustafa had raised a legitimate point. Governor Spencer had not told Horne what to do with the valuable cargo if and when the Marines did seize it. Was that not strange?

Jud left the meeting early to return to the forenoon watch. Horne had divided duty into six watches, joining the first and second dog watches into one stand.

Long hours of raw, fresh sea air invigorated Jud. He was pleased to be free again of land. Shipboard life was the only true happiness he knew—at least, these days.

Life had changed after Jud's wife, Maringa, had died. Tall, sweet-faced, with eyes like a doe, Maringa had been a house slave in the castle of the Omani Sheik All Hadd. Jud had been saving to buy her freedom for the time when she gave birth to their child.

Maringa had brought a son in the world. A Nubian midwife had given Jud an exact description of the child she had delivered, stillborn—Maringa had also died the same night.

In despair, Jud had refused to eat for a week, wanting to die himself, to join his wife and son in a faraway world. But the gods would not have Jud. So he had turned to crime, becoming reckless as he burgled the homes of rich merchants, shops and warehouses, behaving as if he was determined to be caught. He *was* caught, stealing from a warehouse of the Honourable East India Company, and was sentenced to twenty years' imprisonment in Bombay Castle. He would not have cared if it had been a hundred, or a thousand years.

The *Huma*—like the cells honeycombed beneath Bombay Castle—was a world without women. Jud was happy in such a world, at least for the present. At sea, alone on the quarterdeck, or high on the yardarm where he liked to crawl and sit by himself, he talked to his son, speaking to his dead child in the ancient African practice of ancestor worship. But instead of talking to ancestors, Jud talked to his progeny.

"How are you, boy?" he called to the wind.

"Boy, you have a bigger eye than me. Show us how to find that French ship, boy. Help your old man."

Standing on the quarterdeck on the forenoon watch, Jud looked at the southern sky as he talked to his son and, spotting a trace of a storm cloud, he asked, "Boy, what you blowing my way? Is your Ma angry today, boy? Is that your Ma's temper I see rising like brimstone and smoke?"

10

Rendezvous

The **Huma** *grew* restless as morning passed, rising, dipping, lifting on swells, crashing down into the troughs. Overhead, the sky remained cloudless, the sun a yellow blot high on a blue bowl, but all around the frigate the sea churned and thrashed, becoming a greenish-grey murk.

Looking southeast across the bows from the quarterdeck, Horne watched a bank of dark clouds rising on the horizon, forming like a dust storm on a plain. Looking towards the wheel, he saw Groot—a blue peaked cap set back on his tow-blond hair—keeping a wary eye on the clouds.

Jud moved towards Horne. "The storm might move to the east of us, sir."

Horne felt the wind behind him. "Or we're going to blow straight into it."

"Sir, shall we close-roll the topsails?"

Horne remained silent, concentrating on more than wind stretching the canvas; he was listening to the sounds of the ship, her cries, her groans, how supple she was under the growing storm waves. Like people, each ship weathered differently and, as this was Horne's first storm watch for the *Huma*, he was anxious to learn the frigate's each and every eccentricity.

Jud offered, "Sir, why don't I go aloft and send down the pirate?" He and the other Marines referred to the men from the *Huma*'s former crew as "the pirates," calling hands recruited from Company ships "Company jacks" or "jacks," and the new sailors from Madagascar coastal villages, "the lubbers."

The wind pitched the *Huma* more violently, driving her prow into the rollers, intensifying the roll and pitch pattern.

Horne raised his eyes. "It'll be a wild ride up there, Jud."

"Sir, we need a lookout. There's a pirate up now and this weather could toss him over."

Horne agreed. A lookout was necessary, especially so close to the Agulhas current. He knew, too, that Jud enjoyed riding a storm, and would think of any excuse to scale the ratlines.

Lowering his closely shaved head, Jud confessed, "It's this push under my feet, too, sir. A storm troubles me, sir. I'd rather be—" he raised his eyes, "—up top."

Sea turbulence made the deck rise against a man's feet, creating an uneasy feeling. Smiling, Horne waved Jud fore, ordering, "Change course and gallants!"

"Aye, aye, sir." Jud was gone, half-running along the gangway to the foremast, shouting to the pirates, jacks and lubbers.

Horne gripped the quarterdeck rail, noticing men moving from the ship's waist, drawn by the sudden shift in weather, curious to see the change in the sky, the way clouds rose and sped with the wind, their shapes altering quickly as the wind accelerated.

A boiling sea, too, aggravated sea-sickness, and Horne looked to see if any men moved towards the scuppers, doubled over to lose their breakfast.

But the Marines, as well as the new crew, seemed readily reconditioned to sea travel, including the men whom Governor Spencer had gleaned from the Malagasy fishing villages. Horne was less concerned about the ship's provisional crew, however, than he was about the welfare of his Marines.

Neither Groot nor Babcock showed any recurrence of their sickness, nor had it spread to any of the other Marines. Perhaps Babcock had been right. Perhaps Groot's cooking had poisoned them.

The one thing which Horne was most grateful for was that his men were not quarrelsome.

Dissension amongst crew was dangerous. Arguments and fights had been known to sink ships, sow mutinies. Horne had insisted that none of his recruits be pugilistic. He wanted fighters, but not men who fought and squabbled and argued amongst themselves.

Babcock was undisciplined, sometimes bordering on insubordinate and, frequently, downright sloppy. But he had excellent intuition, a keen nose for sniffing out trouble. Fred Babcock was a born survivor and Horne regarded him as one of his best men.

Efficient, fastidious Jingee often irritated the other Marines—Horne had had to face that fact. But Jingee possessed the priceless knack of knowing when to give men elbow room, when to stop nagging his colleagues, how to turn criticism into flattery. Of all Horne's men, Jingee was the only courtier.

Mustafa was probably the most surly-tempered of the Marine unit, the least amicable of Horne's men. Aggressively strong men were often tightly strung, their sensibilities pulled taut like the strings on a musical instrument, ready to snap at the slightest provocation; when played correctly, they produced beautiful music and rendered remarkable results.

Kiro, like Mustafa, was also tightly strung. But, unlike Mustafa, Kiro knew how to keep himself busy. In this respect, Horne identified with him and his constant need to keep his physical drives flowing; always teaching, improving, honing, seeing room to improve oneself, pressing towards an unattainable excellence.

The least difficult man to live and work with was, of course, the African giant, Jud. Kind, generous, quiet, obedient and fearless, Jud had formerly been matched in those qualities by that other affable Marine, Bapu. Ferocious but even-tempered; strong but gentle as a child; vengeful but as sentimental as a new bridegroom—yes, Bapu had been an ideal colleague and companion.

Horne had decided not to try to replace Bapu. He had never set out to assemble any set number of Marines, and had originally chosen sixteen prisoners from Bombay Castle. That number had been pared down to seven. Now there were six.

But should he think about a permanent team, a squadron of a fixed number? Was there a need for a band of saboteurs in warfare? There were Navies. There were Armies. There were Merchant fleets. There were privately conscripted forces which bore arms. But would anyone—any crowned head, democracy or company—require a band of men trained in specialised feats of combat?

Hmmm. It was an interesting idea: men especially prepared for the hit-and-run attacks, a unit never to be disbanded. Or was that why Commodore Watson was maintaining an interest in Horne's motley group of men? Did he have more noble ambitions for the small corps of Marines than Horne even suspected?

His daydreams were interrupted by Jud's cry from the rigging.

Moving fore, Horne saw Jud against the sky, beckoning to him with one hand, pointing southwards, hailing, "Ship ahoy! Ship ahoy!"

What did he see? The *Royaume*?

Forgetting about his idle daydreams of a hit-and-run squadron of troubleshooters, forgetting about the winds tilting the masts and yards, Horne hurried down the gangway and, pulling off his boots, leapt barefooted for the shrouds. The soles of his feet were hardened from walking across rock and sand, and he easily climbed the hemp ratlines toward the forestay, keeping his eyes aloft; he wondered if he had had the good luck to find the French treasure ship so soon.

Clearing the futtock shrouds, he enjoyed the moment of hanging backwards, a spine-tingling suspension in space before resuming his crawl towards the foretopgallant shrouds.

Jud, both mahogany-brown legs locked around the crosstree, raised his right hand, pointing south as Horne approached the yardarm.

Settling against the mast, Horne pulled the spyglass from his waistband, but first accustomed himself to the roll of the ship—a dizzying circle moving left, right, fore, aft—before raising the glass to his eye.

Finding the blur among the distant clouds, he studied the triangle before passing the spyglass to Jud.

Jud held the glass with both hands. "A brig, sir."

Now Horne could see the ship with his naked eye. "That's what I make out, Jud. And a strong gale chasing her."

"With us right behind her."

"Can you catch her colours?"

"I see red, sir, and—" lowering the spyglass, he handed it to Horne, "I can't say for certain, sir."

Horne tucked the spyglass into his waistband and surveyed the horizon. The view was magnificent from aloft, but he would have enjoyed it more without the yardarm circling in mid-air, one moment tipping him to the west, one moment tipping him facedown to the sea, the deck disappearing behind him, and the next moment dashing him backwards to face the sky. The wind was rising, too, and he shouted, "Let's go below."

"If you leave your glass with me, sir, I could stay and try to catch a glimpse of her colours. The wind might help us gain on her."

It was a sensible idea. Brave, too.

Trusting Jud not to put himself—or any of the hands—in danger, Horne passed back the spyglass and swung his leg over the yard, preparing to descend. He was not halfway down the shrouds when he heard Jud beginning to sing, raising his deep, rich voice in a song to the wind. Or, at least, Horne *thought* Jud's words were addressed to the wind, some mysterious African chant carried to the storm clouds gathering on the southern horizon.

His thoughts went back to the ship, and her proximity in the brewing storm.

Horne was nearing the lubber's hole when he heard a shout. Certain it was not part of Jud's song, he tightened his grip on the ratline and looked aloft, to see Jud pointing south, calling, "Another ship, sir! A second ship!"

Scurrying up the ratline, Horne swung onto the cross-tree and grabbed the spyglass from Jud's extended hand. Both legs locked tightly around the yard, he steadied himself with one hand as he raised the glass to his eye.

Yes, there was a second sail on the horizon, a ship which had obviously come from the south towards the first vessel.

Jud shouted over the wind. "She looks like another brig, sir."

Horne was thinking less about the ship's size than about the direction from which she had come. Mauritius lay to the east; the Agulhas current would come from the south-west. Was one ship an escort of the other? Was one the *Royaume* carrying the war chest from Le Havre?

As Horne handed the spyglass back to Jud, a crack of lightning lit the ship.

Ignoring the jagged streak, Jud studied the two vessels. "I see another blur of red, sir," he said. "The second ship's colours look—"

Lightning again streaked the quickly darkening sky.

Horne held out his hand for the glass. "Enough, Jud. We're going down. Everybody. I'm not losing a man to a storm."

"Sir, one question."

"Be quick about it."

"If we see them, sir, they see us."

"I'd think so."

"But the first ship does not appear to be in flight, sir. Not fleeing and not chasing."

"There could be two or three possibilities for that, Jud." Raising his voice above the strengthening gale, he went on, "One, they could be heavily armed. Not frightened of us. Or else they could be heading for an important rendezvous, willing to chance our presence for exchange of information."

"The treasure ship, sir?"

Horne remained silent, not wanting to raise his hopes.

"What are we going to do, sir?"

"Go below," Horne ordered.

"Aye, aye, sir." Jud grinned, grabbing for the shrouds, eyes sharpening for any sign of pirates, jacks or lubbers in the wildly tilting network of masts, spars and rigging.

The Indian Ocean bubbled in the worsening storm, water churning around the *Huma* as she laboured under storm sail. The growing wind whipped the waves into sharp, jagged whitecaps, tossing them into rollers against the frigate's hull as clouds coloured the sky like night, a heavy darkness lit by the occasional crack of lightning.

Horne ignored the rain beginning to pelt the quarterdeck as he puzzled over the meaning of two mysterious ships, of not one but two brigs visible to naked eyesight.

If their meeting was a rendezvous, what was its purpose? Why in the middle of the Indian Ocean? Was it accidental or planned? He knew the two vessels were more than merchant ships—he knew it. He trusted his intuition on that matter. They were not British ships, either, because Company or Navy vessels would raise a flag signal—even to an unmarked ship like the *Huma*.

So who were they? More pirates? Privateers? If so, why hadn't they given chase? Did the *Royaume* have an escort? Or was it in convoy? Would other ships soon be visible? Were they grouping for the storm?

Horne's only consolation was that the two ships—French, Dutch, Spanish, whoever they were—could go nowhere in these foul conditions. The storm came from their direction. The possibility was, though, that they could pass through a lifting storm more quickly than the *Huma*. So Horne had to remain alert, be ready to pounce at the first break in the storm, not losing track of them. If it weren't the French treasure ship, whoever it was might have news of the *Royaume* and be able to give Horne some valuable information.

Pacing the quarterdeck, holding the *Huma* to storm sail, Horne wondered if he was driving the ship too heavily through the gale. He remembered a stormy journey from his boyhood, riding in a coach with his father from Bath to London. His father had told the driver to tie burlap bags over the horses' heads to prevent them being panic-stricken by the lightning. Horne Senior had urged the driver to use the whip on the frightened animals, to force them on in the storm. Young Horne had begged his father to spare the animals, to let them rest, but the elder man had insisted that his appointment in London was more important than any team of coach horses.

Was he himself now doing the same thing? The *Huma* was no animal, of course, but a ship did have a life of its own, it was more than timber and canvas and rigging.

Why, then, was he driving her so ruthlessly into the wind? The main masts had been destroyed recently by gunfire and the replacement and repairs could well have been slipshod. A strong gale would reveal faults, cracks, patchy repairs.

He was troubled by less practical questions, too. He knew that he was uneasy about Governor Spencer's orders, so why was he driving the *Huma*—and himself—like this to obey them? Why was he obsessed with the urge to achieve what might well be impossible? Why did he feel the need to excel, especially in an undertaking which he found suspicious and of which he did not wholeheartedly approve? Was this one of those occasions when obedience might be wrong?

11
Storm Break

The **Huma** *swept* south on the larboard tack, sails cut to storm jib, the rain driving at Horne like small, silver darts as he paced his beloved realm of the quarterdeck. He knew that somewhere beyond the storm wall lay two brigs, one quite possibly the *Royaume* carrying the French war chest, but the cursed storm held him in thrall.

Rollers crashed; foam swept over the bulwarks; the rigging creaked and timbers groaned; Horne was consoled, however, by Jud's topmen—assisted by Babcock's alternative watch—ready to lunge into action at any sudden change of sail.

Lifelines had been stretched for the men to grip as they inched along the thrashing deck, making their way across the wave-swept gangway. Jingee's crew had secured anything loose; Kiro's men had placed blocks under the trucks, a safeguard to stop the guns from breaking loose and careering across deck. Below deck, Mustafa's gang had secured the water casks and stowed all movables.

At the frigate's wheel, Groot stood as helmsman with

a flat-faced mate whom Horne had assigned to him from the *Huma*'s former raiding crew, one of the so-called "pirates." Within easy reach were ropes with which to lash themselves to the wheel should the storm begin to dash them in its turbulence.

Horne's spyglass was useless against the cloud bank. The only thing for which he could be thankful was that the wind was warm and did not chill him. Trusting his bare feet more than leather soles, he had rid himself of his boots, thinking that if men accused Bombay Marines of being buccaneers, why not look and survive like them?

With the rain soaking his breeches and coarsely woven shirt, he considered his alternative course of action. If the storm worsened, he could abandon his plan to lurch his way towards the two ships. Instead, he could bring the *Huma* to the wind. The frigate would make no progress hove-to, but, at least, she might escape storm damage and men's lives would be spared.

Frustrated by being so close to the two brigs, yet unable to close in on them or at least learn their identity, Horne felt blind and crippled on his own quarterdeck. He must find some way to see—if only a short distance. Glancing overhead at the brailed sails and furled canvas, he leapt, barefooted, to the mizzen shroud and climbed towards the mast.

The wind pasted the clothes to his body like a second skin; the rain felt as if it were driving tiny holes into his face; but he clung to the wet hemp, waiting for a break in the storm. If the *Huma* were a bird that never alighted, then in the name of the good Lord Almighty, he would be a willing rider on the tireless creature's back.

·   ·   ·

The flat-faced, wiry young "pirate" whom Horne had assigned to Groot as a mate spoke no English. Neither did he speak the other language which Groot knew—French. As the storm gale worsened, Groot felt a nervous impulse to talk to someone, but having nobody nearby who could understand him, he began speaking his native Dutch to the pirate, unworried that the latter did not know what he was saying.

He first described the house in Bombay where he, Babcock and Mustafa had lived before the press gang had found them, and how Babcock had accused him of poisoning them with his stew of sausages, potatoes and lentils.

"Oh, life there was boring," he said, "waiting for Horne to bring us new orders. But it was not the *schipper*'s fault. He takes his orders from Commodore Watson. What was he to do?"

The pirate's black shoe-button eyes shone in his brown face as he stared at Groot in bewilderment.

"The Dutch name for Bombay is 'good harbour,' " Groot continued, "but to me it was a bad place, a prison. I was so bored there I never stopped talking and worrying and talking more. I don't look like a talkative person, I know. Talkative people are fat and have jolly faces. Me, I am lean and look quiet.

"Babcock, he threatens to pull out my tongue if I don't stop talking. Mustafa, he gets that blank look in his eyes when I talk and he never answers me. Sometimes I think Mustafa has nothing to say. Sometimes I think that inside his head there is nothing but air.

"In prison I talked to myself. I was put into prison for stealing Hyderabad silk. I am not a thief, but I saw a chance to make some money so I took it. If it wasn't for Horne, I'd still be in prison.

"I did not think I was going to like Horne when I first saw him. He's an aristocrat and I knew that fine English aristocrats look down their long noses at the Dutch. They call us cheeseheads. But Horne is not like that. No, the *schipper* is a quiet man. A kind man. A serious man. But a man who likes a good fight. On land, he fights with his hands and his elbows and his feet—anything he can use. And on sea, he fights with muskets and cannon-fire and swords—and anything else he can fight with too.

"Our ship before this was called the *Eclipse*. It was a very fine ship. A frigate, very much like this ship and . . ."

A noise sounded in the distance.

Pausing, Groot held the wheel and looked around him, realising the sound was a hail in English.

Listening more closely, he said, "That was the *schipper* calling. I wonder if he saw the ships?"

At his side, the brown-skinned mate said, *"Als je tijd hebt, Groot, moet je je verhaal nog eens afmaken over je laatste schip."*

Groot stared at him. *"Spreek je Hollands?"*

The man answered, *"Ik ben opgegroeid op Java. Het is m'n moerstaal."*

Groot blushed. The pirate had understood everything he had been saying. Having been raised on the island of Java, his mother-tongue was Dutch.

Horne's first thought was that the outline of the ship was a figment of his imagination, that his eyes were playing tricks on him and he was only seeing what he *wanted* to see. But staring across the starboard bow from his perch in the shrouds, he realised that a break had come in the storm, that the gale had veered the storm clouds from the *Huma*'s path, and he was seeing one of the two mystery brigs making way. But where was the second ship? Had it escaped? Already?

Excitedly, he called as he scrambled down the shroud, "Groot! Prepare to go about!"

"Aye, aye, *schipper*!" came the reply. "Aye, aye."

Back on the quarterdeck, Horne looked aloft, at the sails brailed and furled with double gaskets. Work would have to be fast to put speed into the bird.

"Top ho!" shouted Horne, noticing for the first time that the rainfall had slackened.

Jud appeared on the ratline, a spider across a wet web, quickly putting Horne's commands into actions, bellowing men onto the bulky yards.

Groot, helped by his Javanese mate, both babbling Dutch to one another, held the *Huma* on her new course, waves lapping across deck; the lull in the storm had given the *Huma* the wind gauge and was sweeping her down towards the brig.

Clearly seeing the shape of the brig across the expanse of choppy waves, Horne watched her try to catch the wind for a quick flight. Raising both hands to his mouth, he shouted, "Run out the guns, Kiro!"

As the *Huma* became alive, Kiro's crew rumbled out the guns; Horne held his eye on the sea, searching for the other brig, hoping she was not in some fine position to blast away at the *Huma*. Wouldn't the joke be on him if he sailed into a French trap? A grim, heavy toll such a joke could demand, too!

But, no! There she was! The second brig! She had caught the wind, cutting to the northwest and leaving her sister ship behind.

As the *Huma*'s nose pressed southwest toward the laggard, Horne called, "Prepare larboard guns!"

Having run out the guns, Kiro called for grape shot in the harsh, brittle voice he had used on his *Samurai* students in Bombay. Behind the gun crew men scattered sand, precautions for the gunners on the rain-wet deck.

Snapping open his spyglass, Horne was pleased to see the brig was not catching her stays.

He called to the wheel, "Groot, the helm to larboard!"

A few moments later, Jud's yell came from aloft, "She's not the *Royaume*, sir!"

"Can you see colours?"

"French!"

Lifting the spyglass to his eye, Horne caught the brig's stern and saw the gilt name, *Tigre*. He jabbed the spyglass into his sodden waistband. "Prepare to fire across her bow!" he called.

Treasure ship or not, she would get a warning shot and perhaps worse. Damn it! Where was the *Royaume*? Was she the brig escaping?

As his hand chopped down, the gun flared, a volley shaking the *Huma*; Horne saw the ball's splash in the wind-tossed sea.

Pulling out his spyglass, he studied the brig, now able to see her new tack as well as a view of open gunports.

Not waiting to hear their first roar, he bellowed, "Larboard . . . fire!"

The *Huma* was close enough to the *Tigre* for him to see the fore bulwark explode, splinters flying with the striking volley. A cloud of smoke rose from the *Tigre*'s gun-ports, but her retaliation was as ineffectual as her escape attempt.

Horne felt renewed puzzlement. Was the brig undermanned? Had most of the crew been evacuated to the other brig? Was the ship he was attacking in trouble? Was that the reason for the rendezvous, a distress meeting?

The *Huma* bore down on the brig, moving so snugly that Horne knew a full force from his larboard might more than cripple the *Tigre*. He did not want to capture smouldering timbers.

Looking amidships, he saw Babcock—monkey on shoulder—waiting with his men to participate in any attack that might be ordered.

"Babcock, prepare boarding party!"

Babcock, excited by the prospect of action, returned Horne's wave, answering, "Aye, aye, aye, *aye!*"

Why, Horne wondered, when Babcock *did* address an officer properly, did he do it so annoyingly?

To Groot, he called, "Put helm alee. We're going alongside the enemy."

Excitement rose aboard the *Huma*; in feverish anticipation the men began running for weapons to carry or fire or use as bludgeons.

Horne called, "Boarders, prepare grappling hooks!"

Apart from grapnel, men carried pikes, flintlocks, hammers, axes and lengths of rope to grip as garrottes.

The two ships were nearing, their hulls would soon scrape; pandemonium was spreading across the enemy deck as the *Huma* edged closer, the men waiting to jump from the hammock nettings, to stab across boarding planks.

"Boarders . . . ready . . ."

Horne counted to himself. "One—two—three—" He trumpeted, "Away . . . boarders!"

Shrieking, crying, bellowing, Babcock's men poured aboard the *Tigre*.

12

A Clue

A French officer, his blue-and-gold uniform ripped and stained, shouted to a line of Marines aboard the *Tigre* to raise their muskets and repel the boarders pouring over the rails. The troops fumbled with their weapons, crouching in an uneven row to blast Babcock's men.

Babcock, expecting armed defence from the Marines, threw a grappling hook amidships, its rope catching the line of armed men; the surprise of its touch toppled them backwards, sending their muskets clattering to the deck.

Horne was watching from the *Huma*'s quarterdeck, and noticed that the enemy barely outnumbered Babcock's boarding party. Not wanting to strip the *Huma* of more men, he decided to withhold reinforcements unless it became absolutely necessary to lead a support party. The second brig might reappear and find the *Huma* completely defenceless.

Shouts of confrontation rose from the brig's waist, the clank of sabres, the pop of pistols. Through his spyglass, Horne followed Babcock as he sliced his blade, used the butt of his flintlock, cutting a path towards the poopdeck, the monkey clinging to his neck the entire time.

There was no sign of any officers aboard the French brig except for the ragged young lieutenant. The French Marine unit was small and badly armed, and the seamen raised little or no resistance to the *Huma*'s energetic party of boarders. Horne understood now why the *Tigre*'s gun reply had been so feeble. It was consoling for him to see a minimum of bloodshed.

Catching a flutter of bright colour through the spyglass, he lowered the glass and saw Babcock haul down the French flag, the monkey riding his shoulder.

In a victory whoop which ricocheted between the two ships, Babcock shouted, "Bombay . . . *buccaneers*!"

So the long storm watch had culminated in victory. A partial one, regretted Horne, perhaps even an inconsequential one, for the other brig had escaped and, with it, possibly all trace of the war chest. Had the *Tigre* been tossed to the *Huma* as a diversion? Horne suspected so.

Fred Babcock had acted bravely and loyally. Horne had to admit, however, that the big American colonial was loud, brash when he gave buccaneer war cries, sometimes very obnoxious. Yet Babcock was the obvious choice to command the captured brig which the Marines would keep as a war prize.

With his flintlock stuck into his waistband, his sabre dangling at his side, Horne decided to join the men aboard the *Tigre*. The thought occurred to him that by appointing Babcock to the brig he would be ridding the *Huma* of that wretched monkey.

Leaving Jud in temporary command of the *Huma*, Horne jumped across the grappling lines holding the frigate to the *Tigre* and joined Babcock by the brig's port entry.

Shaking Babcock's hand, he complimented, "Good man. Fine show."

"We did it, eh?"

Horne looked over Babcock's shoulder at the French officer, a thin young man with a straggly brown moustache and sunburnt nose, obviously with no idea who had seized control of his ship.

Babcock nodded at the Lieutenant. "Big shot there don't speak English. Least, he pretends not to."

Horne's knowledge of French was minimal but good enough to make himself understood. Approaching the young man, he decided to identify neither himself nor the unit in any way. The *Huma* purposely flew no flag; he realised, too, that he must caution Babcock about his "buccaneer" cries, that the Bombay Marine should not be connected in any way, not even by slang, with the taking of the French war chest.

In French, Horne began, "Lieutenant, what was the name of your companion ship?"

The Lieutenant held himself upright, more out of fear than protocol, his mouth open, his lower lip quivering.

Horne decided to bluff. "Has the *Royaume* proceeded to Mauritius, Lieutenant?"

The Lieutenant's eyes remained sharp with fear but showed no flicker of recognition at the mention of *"Royaume."*

Horne repeated, "What was the name of the other ship, Lieutenant?"

Receiving no answer from the trembling young man, Horne turned to Babcock. "He's too frightened to speak. Confine him to quarters."

"Why not in bilboes? That'd get some sense from the frog soon enough."

"No. He's an officer, Babcock. Apparently the only one aboard ship."

Babcock cocked his head towards midship, at the motley assembly of African, European and Oriental faces. "What about the rest of them sea rats?"

"Have you made a count?"

"Twenty-three. I reckon the others got away on that first tub."

Horne was pleased that Babcock shared his opinion about what had happened to the rest of the crew.

Babcock added, "Unless there's disease and they died."

Horne had not considered the possibility of sickness aboard the *Tigre*. But the ship did not reek of death or decay; there was no permeating odour of sulphur or some other surgeon's smudgepot and lavations.

Pleased by Babcock's constructive speculation, however, he chose the moment to add, "Babcock, I'd like to take the ship's log to study. That is, if you don't mind."

"Don't mind? Me?"

"I'm placing you in command of the *Tigre*. You've led the attack. You're the obvious man to take charge here."

Babcock lowered his head and pulled one ear, embarrassed and surprised by the sudden appointment.

"Thank you . . . sir."

Horne forced back his smile; it would be unfair to mock Babcock at one of the few moments when he showed a modicum of respect for a commanding officer. Who knew? Perhaps this appointment might be the turning point in his life, might give him respect for propriety. Sometimes a man needed responsibility to pull himself together.

"When we make way, Babcock, we'll follow a south-easterly course."

Babcock brightened. "On the arse of that other ship!"

"Hmmm."

"In this wind, we'll put around easy."

Horne had planned on catching the breeze building.

Babcock lowered his voice. "If I'm going to be captain here for the time being, sir, who's going to be at my wheel? Act as my helmsman?"

Horne had considered this and other details when he had decided to give command to Babcock.

"Groot. He speaks French. His new Javanese mate can come over with him, too. Between the two of them, you should not have any language problem. At least from the wheel."

"Who does that leave you with?"

"I can depend on Jud," answered Horne, impressed with the considerate question. Perhaps Babcock was finally becoming a responsible Marine.

"Fun's fun, monkey," Babcock said to his pet as he stood, head bent, in the cabin of the *Tigre*, the sea slapping against the hull, "but there comes a time when a man's got to give it a rest. The same goes for monkeys."

Crossing to the bunk, he tested the mattress. "Not bad. Feathers."

Rising, he knocked his head on a beam.

"Got to remember that beam, monkey," he mumbled.

He looked around the cabin, rubbing his head and appraising the mullioned stern windows, the brass-cornered lockers, a desk, a glass-fronted book and chart case. "Not bad, monkey," he said, "not bad at all. But we mustn't get used to these comforts, they're not going to last for ever. It could be back to the hammock with us soon enough."

Jumping from Babcock's shoulder, the monkey scrambled towards a mahogany shaving stand, scaled it to the round marble top and, grabbing the shaving brush, put the bristles between his bared teeth.

"Hey! Don't eat that, you stupid monkey! That's a shaving brush! It's mine now!"

Grabbing for the brush, Babcock hit his head on another low beam.

"I'm warning you, monkey," he grumbled, holding his aching head. "If you can't move up in the world, then you—" he thumbed the stern window, "—start swimming."

Etienne Gallet listened to the familiar fall of footsteps overhead on deck. He knew, though, that the men aboard the *Tigre* were strangers, some rough band which had seized control of the French brig.

Sitting alone in his cabin, confined to quarters by the enemy leader, he wondered what he was doing so far away from his family's home in Grasse, away from his mother, his father, and from Oncle Philippe who never came out of his bedroom, but scribbled away until the late hours of the night, writing his memoirs of the War of the Austrian Succession. Was it because of Oncle Philippe that young Etienne had decided to go to sea? Had Oncle Philippe instilled into him an early hunger for adventure with those interminable stories about war and life in faraway countries?

Faraway countries were different once you got there. They had languages you couldn't understand. They were deep in filth which you never seemed to be able to wash off your body. They fed you food which did not stay down in your stomach.

Etienne sighed deeply and ran both hands through his hair. Oh, he would like nothing better at this very moment than to wash his hair. To shave. To put on fresh linen. And to eat some proper food.

What would it be like to sit down in the dining room at home for supper with the family? Delicious roast lamb. Tender potatoes. Freshly baked bread. Hmmm. His mouth watered.

Home was not as distant in miles to Etienne as it was in years. Time. He felt trapped in something called the "present" but which had nothing to do with any of his earlier plans for the future. Since being commissioned in the French Navy, he had come to realise that nothing in life was as you had imagined it would be. Today had been the last straw. He felt depleted. Empty. Absolutely spent.

Captain Le Clerc had abandoned the *Tigre*, sailing away on the *Calliope*. Le Clerc had departed with the valuable iron-banded chest marked for Mauritius. He had clearly left the *Tigre* for the enemy to capture, a crumb to toss to them as he took flight with the precious cargo.

But who were these men who had come aboard the *Tigre*? Were they British? They did not look like British. Not Royal Navy. They wore no uniforms. They flew no flag. Were they pirates? Misfits from every dank corner of the world?

Sitting on the edge of his berth, holding his head in his hands, Etienne Gallet wondered what he would have thought as a young boy back in Grasse if he had known that his fate as the King's Officer would be *this*: to be abandoned by his commanding officer, left as a sacrificial lamb for a band of misfits, together with a small part of the crew aboard the *Tigre*. Le Clerc, the scoundrel, had left in a hurry, too, thinking up his ruse just as the storm had been lifting. Etienne realised that only one thing happened to sacrificial lambs: they were led to slaughter.

But why should Le Clerc have the last word? Or the enemy? Was not this his life? His destiny?

The cabin was dark. The water swirled around the brig in complete blackness. But Etienne Gallet needed no light inside his quarters to find the object he was looking for. He knew exactly where he had left the scent bottle. It had been a farewell gift from his dear mother. Papa had given him a crucifix, and Oncle Philippe a leather-bound diary for making daily entries during his travels. But Maman, dear, sweet Maman, knowing that her rosy-cheeked little Etienne enjoyed the nicer things in life, had given him a crystal bottle of scent. Lilas.

The shatter of the bottle sounded like the tolling of a village bell. The slice of the long crystal shard across Etienne's wrist felt like the cold bite of a Christmas icicle. The blood flowing from his veins felt like water, lovely warm bath water flowing into a zinc tub. And, slowly, a smile on his face, twenty-two-year-old Etienne Gallet died.

13

The Helmsman's Story

The storm passed north towards Madagascar, and the *Huma* and *Tigre* moved eastwards, enjoying brisk gusts, not the tailwinds of a typhoon as Horne had feared.

In the twenty-four hours since Babcock had been placed in command of the captured French brig, Horne had divided the hands from both ships—a total of ninety-one men—into skeletal but adequate crews for the two vessels. Cutting the watches from seven to four, he eliminated both dog watches, creating a middle shift to extend morning, noon and night watches. Babcock followed suit aboard the *Tigre*.

The one serious problem aboard the captured brig was the suicide of its only remaining officer, Lieutenant Etienne Gallet. The brig's crew gave him a sea burial, reading a Papist prayer for his soul.

Horne, thinking of how the young man in the ragged uniform had been too frightened to speak when the Marines had boarded the *Tigre*, closed his eyes and offered the closest thing he could say to a prayer. The death of a weak and innocent man was always sadder than that of a strong one. Why? He didn't know.

Horne was faced once again with the problem of languages, but he hoped he was going to be able to solve it by juggling the crew.

Originally, when he had chosen the men from the cells of Bombay Castle, he had looked for a knowledge of English. Little had he known, those long months ago, that their other languages would serve him on a subsequent voyage. His two crews were a mixture of many nationalities, sharing a wide variety of languages and dialects. Fortunately, however, Groot spoke French and Dutch; Jingee, Kiro and Jud had a knowledge of most Oriental and African tongues; Babcock spoke nothing but English, but Mustafa could understand—and make himself understood—in many of the island dialects offshore from the Ottoman's extensive empire. So far no problems had arisen from language, and Horne told himself that a plethora of tongues could prevent a mutiny taking root and spreading.

Relying on his scant knowledge of French, Horne sat behind his desk in the cabin of the *Huma*, poring over the *Tigre*'s log book, understanding enough to grasp that the captain of the brig, Pierre Le Clerc, had set sail from Mauritius in October for Cape Agulhas.

Le Clerc wrote that his crew complained about not getting enough fish and meat; the helmsman's mate had been flogged for stealing beer; the ship's surgeon had officiated in the capacity of chaplain. Horne learned those things but found no mention of a treasure ship, no details about any rendezvous with the *Royaume* from Le Havre. Le Clerc's voyage appeared to be a simple exploration, making notes of shore lines, observing islands—duties little different from those humdrum activities generally assigned to the Bombay Marine.

Beginning to wonder if the *Huma* might have happened on an innocuous meeting between two French ships at sea, Horne considered the possibility that he had attacked an innocent vessel. Wartime or not, he did not want to travel the Indian Ocean broadsiding French ships at random.

"10 *Novembre*," he read next. On that day, the *Tigre*, passing Cape Agulhas, proceeded towards the Cape of Good Hope, sighting a French ship, the *Elise Sante*, off Cape Town. Captain Le Clerc went aboard to dine with her captain, the Comte de Benoit.

Finding no details of the conversation which had passed between Le Clerc and Benoit during dinner, Horne studied the next entry.

Back aboard the *Tigre*, Le Clerc returned to Cape Agulhas, wishing he could visit Port Elizabeth, wanting fresh fruit and vegetables, but still making no mention of the *Elise Sante* or Benoit.

Jingee, knocking on the cabin door, entered with Horne's midday meal, his brow wrinkled with concern under his turban as he looked for a place to lay a fresh cloth on the cluttered desk.

Horne pushed the French log towards him. "Jingee, you read French. Translate these last few entries for me."

Jingee shook his head regretfully. "Ah, Captain sahib. I speak French. But, no, I do not *read* French!"

Horne thought of his other Gallic linguist, Dirk Groot.

"Jingee, run up a flag signal to the *Tigre*. Tell Babcock that after I have eaten—that *moong dal* smells delicious today—I am coming aboard the *Tigre*."

Jingee's face brightened. Sending signals up the halyard

delighted him. He enjoyed watching the small balls of colour explode into the wind. He could not believe that sixteen small flags had a variation of one hundred and forty-four messages. And Captain sahib had told him that King George's Royal Navy might soon authorise even more for use around the world!

Dirk Groot, blue cap pushed back on his sun-whitened hair, sat at the teakwood desk in the *Tigre*'s cabin and studied the brig's log book. Horne stood anxiously behind him while Babcock slouched against the cabin's low door.

Groot's eyes moved across Captain Le Clerc's intricately written entries, translating as he read, "The ship was rounding Cape Agulhas for Cape Town . . ."

Horne peered over Groot's shoulder. "My French is good enough to understand that much. But I can't find the reason Le Clerc made the journey."

Groot moved to the next line of copperplate script. "He met the *Elise Sante* . . ."

"I understand that part, too," said Horne. "Le Clerc goes aboard the *Elise Sante*. He dines with the Comte de Benoit. But can you find any mention of what they talked about? The reason for their rendezvous?"

Groot flipped the page. Reading, he shook his head, replying, "It doesn't say."

From across the cabin, Babcock called, "Horne, I know somebody who might give you a few answers."

Horne and Groot raised their eyes from the log.

Babcock recrossed his arms. "This morning I thought it might be a good idea to search the men aboard this tub to see if they had any hidden weapons. I ordered everybody to line up on the gangway and strip off their togs."

Horne smiled inwardly, pleased with Babcock's performance as the *Tigre*'s new captain. Temporary command of the French brig was giving him confidence, making him less boisterous, proving him a responsible leader.

Babcock continued. "So there they were, bare arses to the wind, when I noticed a man with a backful of whip marks. Now if I know my sailors, Horne, a flogged man talks quicker than a man with a clean back."

Horne became alert. "Was his name Ury?"

From his seat at the desk, Groot answered, "Aye, *schipper*. Gerard Ury. I took down the name for Babcock."

Horne explained, "Ury's the helmsman's mate."

Groot glanced back across the cabin to Babcock at the door. "Aye. That's what he told Babcock and me."

Babcock, intrigued with Horne's knowledge, angled his head to one side, asking, "Now how in hell, Horne, do you know that?"

Horne gestured to the brig's log in Groot's hands. "Le Clerc mentions Ury in his journal. He ordered him to be flogged for stealing beer."

Babcock grinned. "You get the facts, don't you, Horne?"

Horne frowned. "Not enough, it seems."

Babcock returned to his original suggestion. "So why not bring in Ury? Hear his side of the story?"

Groot reminded Babcock, "The Frenchman doesn't speak English."

"So what?" Babcock leaned back against the teak panelling. "You talked French to him, Groot, didn't you? You can translate for Horne."

Horne liked the idea. "Groot, is your French good enough to carry on a conversation? To ask Ury all the questions I'd want to put to him?"

Groot's blue eyes widened with excitement. "He understood me this morning, *schipper*."

Horne leaned over the desk. "I want you to translate everything I tell you. Even if you know it's untrue."

"Like a trap?"

"More like bait, Groot. I hope that Ury will provide his own trap."

A few minutes later, a lanky seaman with a high forehead and a sunburnt nose stood nervously in the brig's cabin, his back to the bulky desk.

Horne paced in front of the Frenchman, hands gripped behind his back. "Groot," he began, "tell Ury that I've decided to remove all charges made against him by Captain Le Clerc in the ship's log."

Groot translated Horne's words into French; Ury understood and began to protest his innocence.

Listening patiently to the passionate, long-winded reply, Groot finally raised one hand for him to stop.

Turning to Horne, he reported, "*Schipper*, he says he didn't steal the beer. He says he won it from a topsman in a dice game. But he says the topsman is a Corsican pig who lied to Le Clerc and accused Ury of stealing the beer. Ury says he was punished unfairly for a crime he didn't commit."

Horne resumed his pacing. "Tell Ury that I'm forgetting the charges of thievery against him. Tell him I'm wiping the slate clean. Tell him that I'm also dropping the second charge Captain Le Clerc made against him in the log."

Groot turned to the helmsman's mate, translating Horne's words into French.

Ury began shaking his head and protesting as he listened to Groot.

Groot explained to Horne in English, "He says there

are no other charges against him, *schipper*. He says he was punished for one crime and no more."

Horne stepped closer to Ury and began the first part of his fabrication, speaking directly to Ury in English. "Apart from stealing, Captain Le Clerc also charges you with treason in his log, Ury. He writes that you attempted to incite mutiny aboard the *Tigre* after you were flogged. He intends you to be tried by a court of inquiry when the *Tigre* returns to Mauritius."

Groot stood between Horne and Ury, translating Horne's English into French; Ury shook his head, beads of perspiration forming on his leathery brow, insisting on his innocence.

Horne developed the story. "I'm not responsible for what Captain Le Clerc has written, Ury. I only know what I read. The court of inquiry on Mauritius will read the same accusation." Horne reached for the captain's log, holding the bound volume in front of Ury's eyes.

Groot resumed translating, but Horne interrupted, "I shall see Ury gets a fair hearing."

Groot continued as Ury perspired more profusely, shaking his head, repeating he was not guilty of treason.

Horne remained unmoved. He held the log aloft, informing Groot, "Tell him that Le Clerc was obviously under great stress when he wrote these charges in this book. Tell him that Le Clerc was under pressure from his meetings at sea. From the first meeting with the *Elise Sante* off Cape Town, to the rendezvous with the second ship during the storm when we sighted them." Horne opened the book, leafing for the correct page to show the words to Ury.

Groot repeated Horne's statement in French, listening carefully to Ury's impassioned reply, interrupting the

Frenchman to repeat certain words and phrases. At the same time, Horne held out the log for Ury to inspect. But Ury ignored the written entry, convincing Horne that he could not read to check the story's veracity.

Turning to Horne, Groot reported, "Ury says that Captain Le Clerc suffered from no pressures. He says that Le Clerc was in good humour whilst the brig's crew did all the work during the meetings at sea. Le Clerc came from his cabin to supervise a case being transferred from the *Elise Sante* to this brig. Later, during the storm, he supervised the transfer of the same case from this brig to the second ship."

Horne listened carefully to Groot's translation, wondering whether he was finally beginning to understand what had happened between the two French ships at sea.

Setting the log back on the desk, he asked, "Groot, what was the name of the second ship? The vessel we lost in the storm?"

Groot questioned Ury and turned back to Horne. "The ship we saw with the *Tigre* was called the *Calliope*."

"Ask him what was the cargo Le Clerc got from the *Elise Sante* and passed on to the *Calliope*."

Groot put the question to Ury.

The French seaman answered more quickly and freely than Horne had expected, addressing his flow of words directly to Horne.

Groot explained, "*Schipper*, he says many men aboard ship claim there was gold in the case. Money to pay the mutinous French troops on Mauritius. But Ury thinks the cargo had weapons. Pistols and long guns and ammunition."

"Ask him why Le Clerc abandoned this ship to sail off on the *Calliope* with the mysterious cargo."

Groot already had the answer to Horne's question. "Ury's said that the *Calliope* is scheduled to meet another ship. A ship from Mauritius."

Horne became more excited. "Where is that next rendezvous to be, Groot?"

Groot turned to Ury; the French seaman's words were low, and as he said them there was a glint of vengeance in his eye.

Looking back at Horne, Groot said, "He wants to know if you are English and plan to fight Le Clerc if you overtake him?"

Horne fixed his eyes on the helmsman's mate. "If Ury believes we are English and an enemy, why should we not think he is lying to us?"

Groot repeated Horne's question to Ury; after listening, he translated for Horne. "Ury says he's the right arm of the brig's helmsman. He says that the helmsman's a good friend of Captain Le Clerc. Le Clerc and the helmsman drink wine together. He says that Le Clerc tells the helmsman many things which the helmsman passes on to him."

"What he says is true," murmured Horne. "Le Clerc writes in his entries about spending evenings with the helmsman. His name is Claude Dupres."

Moving towards the bullshide map hanging behind the desk, Horne ordered, "Tell Ury to come here and show us where the rendezvous is to take place."

Muttering an oath against Captain Le Clerc, Ury came and stood beside Horne in front of the map.

A meeting to pass the mysterious cargo to another French ship was to take place at Oporto, a small island in the Mascarene Islands to the southeast of Madagascar, southwest of the French headquarters on Mauritius.

Horne explained his theory to Babcock and Groot after he had sent Ury from the cabin. Studying the small indigo speck on the bullshide map, he said, "If Ury's telling the truth—and I believe he is—the French have been passing a valuable piece of cargo from ship to ship, ever since Le Havre. The cargo moved down the Atlantic, around the tip of Africa, and up the Indian Ocean towards Mauritius, being transferred from ship to ship to ship."

"Like a child's game," said Groot excitedly. "Like a game of passing a pebble or a handkerchief."

"Precisely," Horne agreed. "In England we call it 'Pass the Parcel.' "

Babcock pulled his right ear. "That way it doesn't stay on one ship long enough for anyone else to get suspicious about something valuable being there."

"Which is why I suspect the cargo is highly valuable." Horne was growing more confident of his theory. "Such as the war chest despatched from France aboard the *Royaume*."

Turning to the desk, he tapped the ship's log. "Le Clerc doesn't mention the *Royaume* because he never saw her. By the time the war chest reached Africa, it had long ago left the *Royaume*. Le Clerc took possession of it from the *Elise Sante*."

Groot supplied, "And passed it on to the *Calliope*."

"Precisely."

Babcock asked, "So does Le Clerc know it's the war chest he's taken from one ship and is going to pass to another?"

"If not the war chest, then something equally valuable." Horne reminded both men, "Le Clerc abandoned his command—this brig—to sail with the mysterious cargo to the next rendezvous point at Oporto."

Babcock mulled over the theory. "Horne, do you think Oporto might be the last drop point?"

"Before reaching Mauritius, yes."

"If it is the bloody war chest," Babcock went on, "and Oporto's the last dropping point, the escort coming from Mauritius to pick it up could be more than one bloody ship."

"Quite possibly." Horne looked back to the map. "We shall only find out if we get there in time for the transfer."

Groot asked, "What if Babcock's right? What if we get to Oporto and see the entire French fleet? What do we do then, *schipper*?"

"Let's get there first."

14

Boodle's

The clip-clop of horses' hooves echoed through the night along London's fashionable Pall Mall. Towards the end of the cobbled thoroughfare, two lanterns flanked the doorway of a private gaming house known not by its owner's name but, instead, by the name of the manager, a gentleman of society who had lost his fortune and had been forced to earn his livelihood as a professional host—Mr. Boodle.

Apart from cards, dice and other games of chance, Mr. Boodle's house—or, as it was becoming known in society, Boodle's—offered food and a fine selection of wines and liquors. The establishment also provided private parlours for patrons who wished to enjoy an evening in seclusion with their guests.

The late November evening was chilly and a fire had been laid in the hearth of the first floor parlour reserved for Sir Henry Maddox, a frequent visitor to Boodle's and a member of the Honourable East India Company's Board of Directors, the influential group of businessmen known as the Company's Secret Committee.

Dining with Sir Henry Maddox was Sir Basil Rothingham, also a member of the East India Company's Secret Committee, together with two gentlemen from the British Navy Board, Messrs John Todd and Timothy Weldon.

Roast fowl, a joint of beef and game pies had been devoured, pickles, beets and other condiments cleared from their pots; the four gentlemen passed from champagne to port as they began discussing their reason for gathering on this cold autumn evening in a private upstairs dining-room at Boodle's.

Sir Henry Maddox, a round-bellied man, his hair tied in a queue and powdered in the old-fashioned manner, sat back in his armed-chair. "The Company's done its part," he began. "Now it's time for the Navy Board to do theirs, eh?"

The two guests from the Navy Board, Todd and Weldon, sitting side by side on a padded leather bench on the opposite side of the oaken table from Sir Henry and Sir Basil, exchanged cautious glances.

John Todd, the taller of the two, replied, "You've been to the Deptford shipyards, Sir Henry. You've seen the vessels. You may have gathered from what you've seen that we're planning to keep our side of the, ah, arrangement."

Sir Henry Maddox leaned back in his chair, a bumper of port resting on his protuberant belly. "Aye, Sir Basil and I, we've been down to Deptford. We're damned pleased, too, with what we saw. But there's papers to endorse. Provisions to impress. We don't want to part with a shilling till we know the bottoms are ours, clear and dry."

Folding both hands in front of him on the table, John Todd assumed the detached tone of a scrivener. "Sir Henry, when the Navy Board receives word from Leadenhall Street that the Honourable East India Company's Bombay Marines have launched their attack and have been..." he looked at his colleague from the Navy Board, "... successfully annihilated—"

His cold grey eyes returned to Sir Henry Maddox. "Then and only then shall the East India Company have full deed to the six ships the Navy Board has commissioned from the Deptford shipyards."

Plain, simple facts reduced to cold words were more chilling than the November night. The four men were all privy to confidential arrangements made between the Honourable East India Company and the Navy Board; they did not mention the details at the dining-table but the background was foremost in all their minds:

After France had surrendered Pondicherry, the French outpost on the Coromandel Coast, to the British in January of this same year—1761—the war had moved into a stalemate. England could not yet claim victory; France would not budge from India. The British began looking for an excuse to deliver a final blow to drive the French from India once and for all and make it impossible for France ever to re-establish a foothold in the Orient, so leaving all eastern colonies to Britain, all territorial trade there to the Honourable East India Company. But Britain could not appear as the obvious aggressor, not when treaties were yet to be signed, not with war also raging in Canada. The answer came from Le Havre, in the form of a clandestine report that France was dispatching a war chest to pay her mutinous troops on Mauritius. Looking to the Honourable East India Company to perform its share of the work in return for enjoying a trade monopoly, the Navy Board and the East India Company reached an agreement which would lead France into direct conflict, by tricking the French into attacking a private British vessel. The Company's private fighting unit, the Bombay Marine, would be given an order to seize—to *try* to seize—the French war chest, a mission which was a hopeless military cause but politically volatile. The command would come from high in Company ranks, but would later be flatly denied. Who would believe it? Little David had more hope against Goliath than the Company's shabby Bombay Marine had against a French treasure ship. When word came to London that the French had destroyed the Marine ship for no apparent reason, the Navy Board would be applauded for issuing orders to pound the French out of India. The price which the East India Company asked for sacrificing the lives of their Bombay Marines was the replacement of the Company ships which the Royal Navy had pressed into service and lost in battle. Arguments between the Navy Board and the East India Company had been extended for two additional weeks, until the Navy Board recognised that the term "lost in battle" also included ships destroyed by storms while in service to His Majesty's Royal Navy.

Sir Basil Rothingham, a short, meekly mannered man with steel-framed glasses, spoke for the first time since the discussion had begun after the meal. "This entire conversation could have been avoided if Lloyd's did not demand impossible rates to protect ships in war time."

Heads nodded on both sides of the oaken table, the gentlemen agreeing that the insurance agents acting out of Lloyd's Coffee House were becoming avaricious.

The hour was late; all four gentleman wanted nothing more now than to return to their homes.

John Todd, who, living in the distant village of Chelsea, had the farthest to travel, moved restlessly on the padded bench. "So when shall we know if the Marines have been duly eliminated according to our agreement?"

Sir Henry remained the spokesman. "Governor Spencer sails from Bombay as soon as he can verify that the French have slaughtered the Company's Marines and there's solid reason for England to strike back, and strike back hard."

"A long journey, Bombay to Gravesend."

"Not at this time of year, Mr. Todd. The typhoon season's over. If Spencer leaves Bombay in December, he can have word with us in four months."

John Todd persisted. "So the earliest the Navy Board will know is Springtime?"

"I would say so. That gives you time to get word to Pocock's fleet in Calcutta. Colonel Coote's out there, too, with the Army. There will be no problem."

Timothy Weldon, the youngest man in the room, a secretary in the Navy Board and rumoured to be a favourite of Sir William Pitt, sat forward on the bench, asking, "Nobody outside the privileged groups knows of this? Not even the Commodore of the Company's Marine?"

"Commodore Watson?" Sir Henry shook his head, remembering Watson from the West Indies, when he had been Rear Admiral of the Blue. "Watson's looking after his own interest. Retiring soon. Pension, you know."

"Ah!" Young Weldon nodded knowingly. "Pension."

Sir Henry confirmed, "Governor Spencer is giving orders *personally* to the Marine officer. You can rest assured, gentlemen, all will be done very neatly. No leaks to committees or politicians."

"Good. Capital." Weldon rose from the bench; his colleague, Todd, followed him, saying more lightly, "As they say, Sir Henry, it's good doing business with the Honourable East India Company—where the emphasis is on 'Company' rather than 'Honourable'!"

Guffaws and chuckles greeted the popular expression from the commercial world as the four men left the crumb-strewn, port-stained table.

PART THREE
Pawns of War

15

Oporto

The island of Oporto rose like a mountain of grey stone from the Indian Ocean, the morning sun glistening beyond the jagged southern rim as the *Huma* approached on a northwestern course, followed by the *Tigre*.

Adam Horne stood with Jingee and Jud on the *Huma*'s quarterdeck, looking ashore through his spyglass, remembering details from the map.

A small inlet lay on Oporto's southwestern coast; a deeper, wider-mouthed harbour was located on the opposite side of the island. Suspecting that the French would be meeting in the larger cove, Horne planned to anchor his ships on the southern side and send a foot party overland to learn if the *Calliope*—or any other French vessels—lay at anchor.

As hands shortened sails on the frigate, Horne surveyed the grey rocks through the spyglass, following a green trail of vegetation leading down from the island's barren plateau.

"Any sign of life, Captain sahib?" asked Jingee. "Do you see the *Calliope*'s sails?"

"If the *Calliope*'s nearby, Jingee, she's most likely anchored on the far side of the island," explained Horne. "The inlet there is wider and probably provides better shelter from sea traffic."

As he traced the line of vegetation down from the cliff's face, he added, "We must not forget that we might be too late for the rendezvous. The war chest may already have been transferred to the ship from Mauritius. It may now be on its way to pay the French troops."

Jingee's turban glistened snowy white in the morning sun, as he asked, "Which way do you plan to sail around the island, Captain sahib?"

Jingee's enthusiasm for details would normally have pleased Horne, but having lain awake most of the night considering possible confrontations with the *Calliope*, he had risen in a testy mood. The hail of landfall from the masthead had prevented him from shaving, and he stood on the quarterdeck feeling scruffy and irritable.

Lowering the spyglass, he forced himself to be civil. "We shan't make any plans to round the island until a scouting party crosses on foot and brings back details of the far cove."

He handed the spyglass to Jud and studied the island with his naked eye as he explained, "Jingee, you and Groot will be that scouting party. The rest of us will remain aboard ship while you two reconnoitre."

The assignment thrilled Jingee. "Do you think the island's inhabited, Captain sahib?"

"I doubt it. But if settlers or natives do live here, you and Groot know enough languages between you to speak to almost anyone you may encounter. That's why I'm sending you."

His brown eyes wide and alert, Jingee asked, "What should we say if we meet natives, Captain sahib?"

"You both have your wits about you. I am sure you can make up a fanciful story about being traders or fishermen from the mainland, but you must not take any unnecessary chances. The French have allies throughout all the Mascarene islands. You must be constantly on the lookout, too, for a patrol from a French ship."

"Shall we arm ourselves, Captain sahib?"

"Yes. But with no more than a brace of flintlocks and daggers. Don't use the pistols except in extreme danger. A gun shot could alert other ships that we're anchored on this side of the island."

Horne looked at Jud holding the spyglass to his ebony-black face. "Do you see anything?"

"Not a sign of life, sir. Hardly even a tree on the plateau."

"I suspect, Jud, that the island's two harbours are the only reason it appears on a chart."

Studying the stony island through the lens, Jud asked, "Who named it Oporto, sir?"

"The names's Portuguese. They most likely claimed it a hundred and fifty or two hundred years ago, when they first came to India, as a way-station for merchant ships.

"Does your map show how large it is, sir?"

"According to the chart I found aboard ship, it's three miles wide and five miles long."

Jingee stepped forward. "Three miles will be no problem to cross quickly on foot, Captain sahib."

Horne rejoined, "But such a narrow width creates problems for any attack by sea."

Jingee, not understanding, wrinkled his dark brow.

Horne pointed. "Look. See how the island slopes down on the western side. Our masts and rigging might be visible from an enemy look-out as we circled north."

Jud lowered the spyglass. "Aye, sir. You'd have to sail with the gunports open, prepared to fight."

Jingee assured Horne, "I'll keep my eyes open for look-outs as well as the lie of the shoreline, Captain sahib."

Anxious to get his plans worked out before morning had passed, Horne explained the first step to Jud. "Jingee and I will row over to the *Tigre*. Jingee will go ashore with Groot and I'll stay with Babcock to discuss details of the attack. While I'm away, Jud, you're in charge of the *Huma*."

Proud to be honoured in such a way, Jud raised his right arm, saluting, "Aye, aye, sir."

The African giant was one of the few of Horne's Marines to follow Royal Navy conventions. Horne returned the salute, ordering, "Lower the rowing-boat for departure."

Jud descended the companion ladder and moved towards the port entry.

Standing beside Jingee on the quarterdeck, Horne pointed to the green line of vegetation on the island's stony face, explaining that he suspected a creek was there which Jingee could use as a path to follow in climbing to the plateau.

The sun inched its way up the Indian sky, promising a hot day, as the *Huma* and *Tigre* creaked at anchor in Oporto's southern cove. The morning watch had finished by the time Horne and Jingee ascended a rope ladder to the port entry of the *Tigre*. Horne carried a parchment chart tucked into his waistband.

In readiness for the meeting, Babcock had stretched an awning across the brig's quarterdeck as protection against the sun. Locking the monkey in his cabin, he had brought up two chairs to the quarterdeck so that he and Horne could enjoy the cool breeze blowing off the sea.

Before joining Babcock, Horne stood with Jingee and Groot by the port entry, emphasising what landmarks they should look for on the island, reminding them not to fire their pistols unless they were in extreme danger.

Watching the snub-nosed boat move silently from the brig to the rocky shoreline, he waited until he had seen the two men hide the boat behind some boulders and find a route up the craggy face of the island. Satisfied that they were on their ascent to the plateau, he turned to join Babcock.

As the breeze flapped the blue awning, he sat down facing Babcock. There was one thing he wanted Babcock to understand immediately. "We can't make a definite plan until we know if the *Calliope*—or any other French ship—is on the other side of the island."

Babcock added, "Or no ships at all."

Babcock's carefree attitude relaxed Horne's gruff mood. "I think we can safely act on the premise that the French will keep to the pattern of passing the war chest from ship to ship . . . that is, if it *is* the war chest they're passing."

"What you're saying, Horne, is that we don't know a damn' thing."

"Correct. But if we don't take a few chances and try to make a few deductions, we won't achieve anything."

Leaning forward in his chair, he studied the chart which

he had spread out on the deck, weighting the four corners
with stones. "The *Huma*'s more heavily armed than the
Tigre. Therefore, I'll take the northern route whilst
you . . ." he pointed at the island's lower boundary, ". . .
sail the southern coast."

Babcock followed Horne's finger. "The southern
route's shorter."

"In distance, yes. But don't forget the reefs. They're
going to slow down your progress considerably."

Babcock wore no shirt and had cut off his *dungri* trousers at the thigh. Sitting sideways in his chair, one bare
leg slung over the arm, he looked more closely at the
chart. "The chart I've got down in the cabin gives better
details of the reefs than this one. Shall I get it?"

"No. This map has a larger sketch of the other harbour.
That's what we must concentrate on now. You and Groot
study your chart in your own time to learn your way
through the reefs."

Pointing at the northern cove, Horne continued. "After
you clear the last reef, make for the southern promontory
of the harbour mouth. If you see more than one ship, lure
it away so that I can sweep down from . . . here." He
pointed to the upper half of the harbour's wide entrance.

"What if there are two ships and they both give chase?"
asked Babcock.

"Head out to sea. I'll see you leaving and will know
what's the matter. We might be able to trap them between
us, or we might have to take flight, but I doubt whether
the ship carrying the war chest will go in pursuit if there's
a second or third ship to give chase for her."

"What if there's more? Like the whole fleet?"

Horne took the question seriously. "We can tackle two.
Three at the most. But if you see four or more ships, make

north and we'll rendezvous near Réunion." He pointed at the island located to the northwest.

Babcock turned back to Oporto, studying its northern harbour. "Too bad there's no way we can move guns overland from here and fire down on top of the buggers." He looked at the rocky cliffs surrounding the cove, adding, "Especially if the shore's high like this one."

Horne considered the suggestion. "That's good, Babcock. Extremely good. The only problem is time. It's too late to dismantle cannon and pull them across the island. Until Groot and Jingee return, we don't even know what it looks like."

Babcock pulled his ear. "Isn't there something we could use to bombard the bastards? Rocks? Fire balls? Some little exploding surprises?"

Horne repeated, "Let's wait to hear what the island looks like and take it into consideration with our available time."

Babcock leaned back in his chair, locking both fingers behind his neck. "Horne, answer me a question," he drawled. "How likely do you think it is that Ury may not be telling the truth? That he may be lying about the French passing cargo from ship to ship?"

Horne did not hesitate. "My intuition says Ury isn't lying."

"Let me ask you another question." A smile played on Babcock's lips. "What does your intuition tell you about the East India Company sending the Marines on this wild goose chase in the first place?"

Horne was pleased that Babcock had asked such a question. He was putting a great deal of trust in the American colonial and felt glad that he was not accepting duty blindly.

By nature, though, Horne disliked being questioned. It made him uncomfortable to be asked to divulge his thoughts and opinions, especially if they concerned a Company assignment. He had spent most of the previous night wondering why Governor Spencer—and not Commodore Watson—had given him the orders to commandeer the French war chest, and it still puzzled him that the Marines should have had to sail to Madagascar to receive orders from the Governor of Bombay.

The blue awning flapped gently in the breeze. Horne answered, "I've learned that when a man tries to understand the ways of the East India Company, he only becomes more confused. I try to obey commands and not ask questions."

"Duty means everything to you, doesn't it, Horne?"

Horne looked back at the chart. "Almost everything, Babcock. And in pursuit of present duty, we can only make provisional plans and keep our men ready and alert. So let's get on with it."

His voice hardening, he ordered, "Now to discuss crew."

Horne's meeting with Babcock concluded with an assignment of watch duties aboard both ships. Horne reminded Babcock not to allow the men to venture from ship, not even to go swimming or to cool themselves in the cove.

Descending the ladder from the quarterdeck, he paused when he saw a lanky seaman with a sunburnt nose approaching.

In French, the man asked, "May I speak to you, sir?"

Horne recognised Gerard Ury.

Ury's manner to Horne was respectful, his French slow and clearly enunciated, so that Horne could understand him. "My friends are worried, sir, that Captain Le Clerc has written false charges against them in the log, as he did against me."

Horne flinched. Was his fabrication coming home to roost?

Drawing on the little French he knew, he replied, "Tell your friends, Ury, they have no reason to worry if they remain loyal to me."

Ury raised his eyes to the rock cliffs rising around the two ships in the cove. "This is Oporto, isn't it, sir? Where Le Clerc is meeting the ship from Mauritius and the cargo is being passed for the last time?"

Horne thought quickly. "If the French come to this cove, Ury, you will know as soon as the rest of us."

He dismissed the lanky seaman with a curt nod.

Watching Ury slouch back to his friends near the mizzenmast, Horne knew he must be extremely wary of the French seamen. They could easily mutiny or abandon ship. If they suspected that French support was close at hand on the other side of the island, they might raise a hue and cry, betraying the Marines' presence on Oporto.

16

The Trouble with Lying

Acting on Horne's orders, Babcock divided the *Tigre's* watch into three groups for the ships' wait in the south cove. Concentrating on separating the French seamen from one another as much as possible, he spread them throughout the brig. Standing by the coaming with Mustafa, studying a small group of white- and brown-faced men holystoning the deck amidship, he repeated Horne's warning, "Keep your eyes on the frogs."

Mustafa rested one hand on the flintlock tucked into his waistband. "What's the trouble?"

"Horne says to be on guard."

"The Frenchies are threatening us?" Mustafa's other fist tightened on his rope garrotte.

"They might give away our position if they thought their ships were on the other side of the island." Babcock looked astern to the second group of seamen. They were mostly Lascar sailors recruited for the *Huma* in Port Diego-Suarez. They were supervised by the Asian, Dangi, whom Babcock had appointed as a temporary leader.

Mustafa grunted. "I trust none of these pigs."

Six months of living with Mustafa in Bombay had taught Babcock that the thick-chested Turk was suspicious by nature. He cautioned, "Don't go looking for trouble, Ugly. Just be ready if it comes."

Mustafa frowned. "What are Horne's orders . . . Big Ears?"

Babcock raised his eyes to the men in the rigging. "To wait until Groot and Jingee get back with a report from the other side of the island, and then either to blast the frogs to Kingdom Come or to high-tail it back to Bombay."

Mustafa showed more curiosity. "We might have a fight soon? What does it depend on?"

Babcock looked at the surrounding cliffs. "How many ships might be on the other side of the island."

Mustafa frowned. "Probably none."

Babcock glanced over the brig's larboard. Horne's rowing boat had reached the *Huma* and the Captain was beginning his climb to the port entry.

Turning to Mustafa, he explained, "Horne says we'll take on three ships, but no more. In the meantime, there are reefs to worry about. I'm going below to study my chart before Groot gets back." With a last look at the brig's three groups of men, he added, "If there's trouble, give me a shout or whistle. Whatever you do, Ugly, don't fire your bloody pistol unless you absolutely have to."

Mustafa raised his garrotte. "I can take more men with this than you can with a gun."

"Be ready to prove it."

Babcock ambled away from Mustafa, stooping as he climbed down the companionway towards his cabin.

Descending the narrow wooden rungs, he brooded

again about Horne's plan, wondering if Groot and himself could navigate the brig through the reefs in time to reach the other side of the island before Horne got there on the northern route.

Reaching for the door handle, he thought of Horne's orders that he should lure away any escort vessel from the ship carrying the war chest.

He opened the cabin's door and his mind went blank. His monkey was squatting on his desk, sitting amid a drift of torn paper. It was holding a shred of parchment to its mouth, a white scrap which Babcock instantly recognised as part of the chart plotting Oporto's southern reefs.

Gerard Ury crawled slowly across the deck of the *Tigre*, scraping the abrasive holystone over the planking as he listened to four other Frenchmen speaking in low voices.

Below the nettings, a moon-faced seaman from Marseilles, Alain Folinguet, whispered, "Who do we stand a better chance with? The Englishman or Captain Le Clerc?"

Jean Polaire from Cherbourg answered, "I say we should stick with Le Clerc. Better the devil we know."

"But Le Clerc abandoned us to the enemy," protested Folinguet. "He also accused Ury here of treason. Do we want to trust ourselves to a madman like that?"

Polaire moved closer to Gerard Ury. "Did you read Le Clerc's actual words in the log, Ury? Did the Englishman show you the entry that accuses you of treason?"

Gerard Ury was illiterate. But rather than remind the others that he could not read or write, he raised a matter which he believed to be more important than the log.

"We must learn who these men are before we try to

escape from them," he answered. "They might help us as they promised."

The fourth Frenchman in the group agreed. "Ury is right. These men may not harm us. I spoke to one of the yellow sailors from Madagascar. He says none of these seven men belong to the British Navy. He says they fight for money, that they are soldiers for pay."

"Pirates," whispered Polaire. "What good can pirates do us? Do you want to sail under the black flag?"

"They may at least takes us back to Mauritius as they promise," Folinguet argued. "Then we can state our side of the matter to a council without having Le Clerc or his log accusing us of crimes we didn't commit."

"Shhh." Ury glanced at the approaching Mustafa. "Here comes the big bear."

The Frenchmen fell silent as Mustafa stalked round them, slapping the rope garrotte against his trouser leg, flailing it like a whip as he passed the men's naked backs.

As the morning sun blazed up the Indian sky, Horne paced the *Huma*'s quarterdeck, impatient for Groot and Jingee to return with their report. They had been gone for no more than two hours.

He was troubled, too, by Ury asking him if Le Clerc had accused other men of treason in his log. Would they ask to read it? In all fairness, such a request would not be out of order, Horne thought, but of course, he could never consent to it.

Feeling the stubble on his face, he wished he had not lied to the French seaman about the mutiny charges. The prevarication had achieved the desired results, but lying was dangerous. It imperilled men's loyalty. Responsible leaders, Horne had learned many years ago, never lied to their men.

He remembered the first lessons in leadership he had received from Elihu Cornhill. Cornhill's schooling had come at a time when Horne had needed every shred of help he could get. The senseless murder of his fiancee had left him despondent, totally without hope or confidence, sceptical of all moral values.

Horne had been a few years older than most of the other young men studying with Cornhill on the derelict estate. The majority of the old retired soldier's protégés had been in their teenage years, many from squalid city ghettoes and some little older than urchins. Cornhill preferred students who had had some brush with crime. His motto had been: *Grab a young criminal early in life and you might find a soldier.*

Horne looked up at the morning breeze teasing the frigate's furled sails, and remembered how Cornhill's lessons had involved mental as well as physical training. Elihu Cornhill had gathered much of his philosophy of warfare from Canadian campaigns. Returning to England, he had brought back the unorthodox ways of North American Indians, hoping to create a new breed of soldiers, using camouflage, scouting, dawn attacks.

He had taught his students that a soldier must know himself before he tried to understand the enemy. He would order a pupil to stand for hours in front of a looking-glass, listing aloud his best qualities, discussing with himself how he might improve his weaknesses. He had warned, however, that the student should close his eyes if the reflection became too intense and uncomfortable. A man could endanger his mind with too much self-questioning.

Horne remembered a night on which he had stood in front of a looking-glass in his room in the dilapidated manor house. He had blackened his face with soot for a midnight excursion through the forest and had been studying his reflection.

Gazing back at him, he had seen a total stranger. Feeling a new, unfamiliar strength inside him, he had understood for the first time why thieves and footpads wore masks. More than hiding identity, a mask gave power. Faceless men took greater risks.

Was that why, to this day, he resented people asking prying questions about his personal life? Was that why he guarded details about his past from inquisitive people? Because he had learned the value of secrecy? Or was he overly protective? Was he wrong to keep everyone at arm's distance?

A splash distracted Horne's introspection.

Looking toward the *Tigre*, he saw a figure surface from the waves. As the man began to swim strongly towards the *Huma*, Horne remembered that he had distinctly told Babcock not to allow his men in the water.

He stepped to the rail, wondering who it was. What had happened? Why was someone breaking his order?

Then he saw that the swimmer was Babcock.

17

North Cove

The dull scratching of cicadas cut the morning's stillness as Jingee and Groot lay flat-bellied in the dry grass above the north cove. Peering down over the rocky cliffs, the two Marines watched a rowing-boat glide from a two-masted ship to the sandy shore.

Through a spyglass, Jingee studied the brig's name painted on the stern. He whispered, "The *Calliope*'s the French ship which escaped Captain sahib in the storm."

Groot took the spyglass from Jingee and inspected the vessel. Moving the glass inshore, he could see men splashing in water, their voices unintelligible in the distance.

Focusing the glass back on the ship, he said, "There can't be more than fifty men down there."

"Captain Le Clerc must be one of them," said Jingee, appraising the coastline to report to Horne.

"Do you think they're waiting for the rendezvous?" asked Groot. "Or do you think they've already passed the war chest—"

He stopped. He rose to his knees, looking through the spyglass.

"It's there. The war chest. I can see men with muskets standing around a big box on deck."

Jingee snatched the spyglass from Groot's hand.

Anxiously, Groot whispered, "Let's creep down farther for a better look."

Jingee shook his head, the spyglass to his eye. "No. We're close enough to see."

"But we might hear something," Groot argued. "You can go in one direction. I can go in another."

"No," Jingee repeated more firmly. "We must do exactly as Captain sahib told us to do. We've looked. We've seen how many ships are here. We've studied the terrain. Now we must return to the *Huma* so that Captain sahib can make his plans."

A loud blast shattered the morning's stillness.

Groot jumped, his eyes darting all around him on the precipice. "What was that?"

Jingee lay in the tall grass, surveying the rocks through the spyglass. He stopped when he saw a puff of blue smoke rising from a stone promontory protruding like a finger out into the sea.

"A cannon." Jingee handed the spyglass to Groot. "Le Clerc has moved a cannon ashore for a look-out station."

Groot turned the glass to the sea. Spotting a white fleck on the horizon, he nodded. "You're right. It's a ship. The cannon's signalled the arrival of a ship."

Jingee saw the sails billowing from a three-masted vessel in the distance. "It's come from the northeast. That's where Mauritius lies. It's come for the war chest."

Groot did not reply.

Eager to get back to the *Huma* to report to Horne, Jingee urged, "We must not waste a moment. We must run back and tell Captain sahib he's got time to surprise the Frenchmen's rendezvous."

When Groot still did not answer, Jingee turned his head and saw the tip of a bayonet jabbing at Groot's throat: a French Marine stood behind them, a musket in his hands.

Jingee's reaction was immediate.

Yanking the knife from his waistband, he rolled backwards and sprung like a cat for the soldier's back. Locking both legs round his chest, he clung tightly as he sliced the blade across the French Marine's throat.

The Marine's musket clattered to the ground; he pulled at Jingee's arm; he pushed at the bare legs locked around his chest; he struggled against Jingee's crab-like hold until warm blood began flowing from his neck, a dark red river gushing from his throat, and he folded limply onto the ground.

Groot stared, mesmerised.

Jingee scrambled from the corpse, studying the blue-and-red uniform. In a whisper, he reported, "He can't be alone. There must be a patrol about, exactly as Captain sahib warned us."

Groot remained motionless, staring at the Frenchman. "He's . . . dead."

Jingee had spotted another armed Marine across the parched ridge. Ignoring Groot's state of shock, he pushed him flat to the ground and raised himself to grass level, his small brown eyes alert for more men on guard patrol.

Seeing no one, he wiped his bloody knife across the grass and tucked it back into his waistband. "If they find this body," he whispered, "they'll know we're here. Cover him with grass and earth. Work quickly. I'll go and get the other one."

" 'Get' him?" repeated Groot, aghast.

Jingee nodded, eyes surveying the terrain.

"You're going to . . . *kill* another man?"

Jingee nodded again. "Be ready to run back to ship. I'll signal when it's safe to stand. We'll meet over there, by that old twisted black tree."

Groot swallowed nervously, his throat dry.

"Listen for a bird call and start running," Jingee instructed.

Groot shook his head.

Jingee was gone.

Alone with the dead soldier, Groot glanced from the corpse to the direction in which Jingee had disappeared through the dry, brown grass.

Raising his head, he looked at the second Marine, watching him turning now this way, now that, obviously searching for the other man in his patrol.

Hurrying with his work, Groot covered the corpse with handfuls of grass and earth. As he camouflaged the makeshift grave, he thought how quickly everything had happened. One minute, he and Jingee had been looking at the three-masted ship approaching in the distance; the next minute, he had felt the bayonet against him. Jingee had sprung upon the soldier as fast as lightning, totally unafraid of his weapons.

Groot remembered that the little Tamil had been condemned to the underground prison of Bombay Castle for murder. He had used a knife in killing an English employer.

Pausing in his work, he raised his head above the grass and looked in the direction of the other Marine. He was no longer there.

Had Jingee already struck?

• • •

Jingee bellied his way through the tall grass, mindless of the stones scratching his skin as he continued towards the French patrolman who was scanning the landscape for his companion.

His heart beating with excitement, Jingee gripped the dagger in his right hand, using his elbows to propel himself.

Stopping, he raised his head to see how far to the left or right the patrolman had moved. As he scooted to the next large boulder, he saw the patrolman turn towards him; the Frenchman was close enough for Jingee to see that he was young, a faint trace of a brown moustache on his upper lip.

For the first time Jingee considered what he was about to do, and what he had already done.

Murder. The word did not frighten him; not when the man he had killed—and the one he was about to kill— could easily murder him.

Hidden in the dry grass, he knew that if he thought too much about the heinousness of murder, he might hesitate and fail. He also knew that he could not risk merely tying and gagging the patrolman. Escape could jeopardise all of Captain sahib's plans.

Jingee sprang like a cat. His bare legs gripped the patrolman's arms as he clenched his arm around the young man's neck, the knife deftly slicing the skin. He increased the pressure to cut the arteries and slice the jugular vein, releasing a warm gush of blood.

18
Last Orders

Horne listened without interruption to Jingee's and Groot's report. When they had finished, he asked, "What did you do with the bodies?" He stood facing them on the *Huma*'s quarterdeck.

Groot's face was smudged with dirt and his cap dotted with burrs. "I scooped earth over the first one and covered it with grass and sticks, *schipper*."

Jingee's white turban was dirt-stained and scratches covered his legs, chest and arms. He showed none of Groot's nervousness about the killings.

Proudly, he reported, "I surprised the second patrolman as his friend surprised us, Captain sahib. I opened his throat before he could guess what was happening. Then I rolled the body into a ravine and covered it so that nobody will ever find it."

Nearby on the quarterdeck, Babcock stood wearing only his cut-off trousers, the sun drying them after his swim from the *Tigre*. Gone was his usual brash, boastful manner. He was still humbled from confessing to Horne that his monkey had eaten the *Tigre*'s charts, destroying the navigational chart of Oporto's reefs.

Horne ignored Babcock, concentrating on Jingee and Groot. "Which way's the wind?"

Jingee stepped forward. "To the south, Captain sahib. I remember which way the smoke blew when the cannon fired."

Horne clasped both hands behind his back, considering the information in terms of the provisional plans he had made with Babcock. The news that Babcock's monkey had destroyed the charts had added to his irritability. Unshaven, his forehead furrowed, he fought to control his temper. "We'll move out in three groups. Two sea groups and one overland patrol."

Resuming his restless pacing, he looked at Jingee and Groot. "While you two were away, Babcock suggested using a land attack. From what you tell me about the cliffs on the other side of the island, they're tall and rocky enough for a patrol to create a useful diversion. Jingee, I want you to lead such an attack."

"What kind of diversion, Captain sahib?"

"I'll explain in due course," he snapped. "In the meantime, I want you to think which men you can recruit for your patrol. Choose men with no particular skills aboard ship and make certain none of them are French. We cannot risk anyone betraying your position on shore. Also, choose no more than eight men for the patrol. Manpower remains at a premium."

"Yes, Captain sahib." Jingee bowed from the waist, hoping to break Horne's crusty mood with his attentive manners.

Horne looked at Groot. "How well do you remember the reefs?"

Groot's head was held as if he were in a formal naval inspection. Stiffly, he replied, "*Schipper*, I looked at the *Tigre*'s charts last night when I came off watch duty. But I must study them again before we depart, so that I can refresh my memory."

"That's impossible."

"*Schipper?*"

"The charts have been destroyed, Groot."

"Destroyed?" Groot looked at Babcock.

Horne paced back and forth. "Although my chart does not detail the southern reefs, you can study it, Groot, before you return to the *Tigre*, if that will help you in any way."

Still confused, Groot asked, "How was the *Tigre*'s chart destroyed, *schipper*?"

Babcock stepped forward from his starboard position. "With all due respect, Horne, it was my fault, so I think I should explain."

Horne waved a hand for Babcock to proceed.

Turning to Groot, Babcock said, "I locked my monkey in the cabin while Horne and I had a meeting this morning on the *Tigre*. Like a fool, I left the chart on the desk and that pesky monkey . . . ate it."

Jingee gasped.

Lowering his head, Babcock proceeded, "That's what I'm doing here. I swam over to tell Horne the bad news. Also, I came to say that I remember the reefs fairly well, so—"

Horne interrupted. " 'Fairly well' isn't well enough, Babcock."

Babcock hung his head. "I realise that—" adding uncharacteristically, "—sir. But I remember how the reefs divided into three fingers, like—" He held up his right hand, pronging his thumb, index and middle finger.

Horne's ill-humour was not tempered. "Babcock, I'd rather change our plans now if you're not one hundred per cent certain about the reefs. The *Tigre* doesn't have the gun power of the *Huma*. Nevertheless, you could sail the northern route and let me trust my memory with the reefs."

Groot stepped forward. "*Schipper*, I remember the reef's three fingers. Between Babcock and me, we can cross them."

Horne's tone was severe, threatening. "I'm taking you two men at your word."

"Aye, *schipper*." Groot glanced nervously back at Babcock.

"Very well." Horne turned to Jingee. "Begin selecting the men from the *Huma* you want to take in your patrol, before you return to the *Tigre*."

To ingratiate himself with Horne, Jingee salaamed as he bowed. "Yes, Captain sahib."

Horne said, "Babcock's named the East Indian, Dangi, as a subordinate in your absence, Jingee. The man knows nothing about ships but he seems trustworthy. I suggest you take him."

Jingee was not pleased with the suggestion but, not wanting to cross Horne, he salaamed, answering, "As you wish, Captain sahib."

Looking astern at two rowing-boats circling the *Huma* and *Tigre*, Horne said, "Both ships will maintain the same division of Marines. Groot and Babcock, you sail with Mustafa. I keep Jud and Kiro."

Babcock nodded; Groot touched his cap, replying, "Aye, aye, *schipper*."

Horne pointed to the open boats as the men inside them

tied tow lines to both vessels, and ordered, "Now make those men put muscle into their oars. This is it. So let's catch that damned wind."

The hour was approaching noon; the day was November 30, 1761.

19

Bombay Castle

In the harbour city of Bombay, on November 2, Commodore Watson visited Governor Spencer in Bombay Castle.

Puffing, dabbing his jowls in the heat as he climbed the stone stairway to Governor Spencer's office two storeys above his own, Watson was ostensibly welcoming Spencer back to Bombay from his voyage to Madagascar. The true purpose of the morning call was to hear details of Spencer's dispatching Adam Horne to capture the French war chest.

Watson did not consider Spencer a close friend. The two men did not meet socially; their wives did not exchange invitations. The Spencers associated with the aristocracy; the Watsons were homely people who preferred talking about kitchen gardens and grandchildren rather than court gossip.

Governor Spencer sat behind a gold-cornered table in his vaulted office, looking dignified, even imperious, in a highbacked chair; the intricately carved lozenge of the

Honourable East India Company's crest, "HEIC," was
visible over the top of his softly marcelled grey hair.

Thanking Watson for calling upon him, Spencer proceeded. "I'm pleased to say that your man, Horne, arrived
safely in Madagascar."

Watson was relieved that Spencer was wasting no time
in addressing the main concern. "I sent Horne and his men
on the Indiaman as you instructed, Your Excellency."

Spencer kept his prosaic tone. "I'm afraid, Watson,
there was a spot of trouble on the voyage to Diego-
Suarez."

"Trouble?" Watson stiffened.

"The *Unity* was attacked by pirates," explained Spencer. "Captain Goodair was wounded and one of Horne's
men killed."

"Killed? Good God, who?" Watson knew how close
Horne had become to the band of men he had recruited
from prison.

"I can't remember the man's name. I think it was one
of the Indian chaps." Spencer waved his hand dismissi-
vely. "The point of my story is that Captain Goodair was
wounded and, because his First Mate had been taken ill
at the journey's outset, there was no competent man to
take command during battle."

Watson sat forward, fearing the worst. "Don't tell me
that Horne overstepped his bounds and assumed command
of a . . . merchant ship?"

"Quite the contrary. Command fell upon the shoulders
of the Second Mate, a young man named Tree. Thanks to
Horne's careful and, I understand, unassuming advice,
Tree captured the two pirate ships, claiming a major victory for the *Unity*."

Watson relaxed back into his chair, beaming like a proud father.

"Hearing of the victory," Spencer continued, "I assigned the larger of the two prizes to Horne. As the Navy will be giving him no support in his assignment, I thought he should at least have a decent ship."

Watson gripped his handkerchief, asking apprehensively, "The Navy's not supporting Horne at . . . any point?"

"Of course not." Surprised at the question, Spencer knitted his brow. "You know the assignment's solely for the Bombay Marine."

Watson dabbed beads of nervous perspiration from his bald plate. "But, Your Excellency, I presumed . . . I presumed . . ." He faltered. He no longer knew what he presumed. His mind had been bogged down with guilt since he had sent Horne and his men off on the merchant ship to Madagascar. He was ashamed that he had not demanded that Governor Spencer tell him more about the war chest assignment. He chastised himself for not having put his commission on the line when the Company had failed to give him details. Why should Horne be in jeopardy and he himself be sitting safely in Bombay Castle?

At the risk of being paid off, Watson resumed where he felt he should have begun six weeks ago.

"Why did you give orders to Horne, Your Excellency?" he asked. "The responsibility was mine."

The blunt question startled Spencer. "Because *my* orders came directly from Company headquarters. From Leadenhall Street."

"But Bombay Marines are under my control."

Governor Spencer kept his voice calm. "Commodore Watson, must I school you in Company organisation? The

Bombay Marine comes under the direct authority of the Company's three Governors—Governor Pigot of Madras, Governor Vansittart of Bengal and myself here in Bombay. We three Governors can even disband the Marines if we so desire."

Watson ignored Spencer's thinly veiled threat. "But men's lives are at stake, Your Excellency."

Spencer held his head aloft. "As is peace between England and France."

"Don't you understand, Your Excellency? Dispatching Horne and handful of ragged boys to commandeer a French treasure ship could be sending them on a suicide mission?"

Spencer shifted uneasily in the carved chair. "First of all, Commodore Watson, Adam Horne's men are hardly a band of 'ragged boys.' "

Watson became more heated. "Good God, sir. They're certainly not tried and true soldiers. They're brigands with little more than one foot out of gaol."

"A fact you yourself, Watson, convinced me was an asset when I agreed to Horne's recruiting that scum from prison earlier this year."

"For a completely different assignment," Watson reminded him.

"Which they performed most efficiently."

"If you have so much faith in them, sir, why all the secrecy now? Why keep details from me as you have been doing? Why isolate me from my men? Why give Horne orders in Madagascar when I'm back here in Bombay?"

"Need I remind you, Commodore, that we're at war? That certain precautions must be taken?"

"Who's at war?" snapped Watson, impatient with Spencer's lofty attitude. "The East India Company? Or England?"

Spencer's lips thinned with his voice. "The East India Company *is* England."

"That's reassuring to hear. I was beginning to think that England was nothing more than the Company—with the Company too often playing God."

Spencer's slight frame stiffened in his chair. Reaching for a quill on the table, he began toying with it nervously. "Watson, may I caution you about saying something you might later regret."

Watson rose. "Your Excellency, the only thing I could ever possibly regret would be the senseless loss of men. Too often I've seen the Company treat human life as if it were nothing but more noughts on their accounts sheet."

Spencer rose too, his face red. "I suggest we resume this conversation later. When you have better control of yourself, Watson."

"I have perfect control of myself."

"Commodore, good day. I have work to do."

"As I do. I bid you good day, Your Excellency."

Turning, Watson stormed out of the Governor's chamber.

"The old fool." Left alone, Governor Spencer sat nervously chewing his fingernails.

Why should Watson start causing trouble at this late date? The last thing the East India Company's Secret Committee wanted now was for someone of Watson's rank to arouse the public's suspicions. Horne and his men had been sent to their slaughter, and nothing could, or should, be done to revoke the order.

Spencer had been back in Bombay from Port Diego-

Suarez for less than twenty-four hours, but already he was anxiously waiting for a report that Horne's ship had been sunk, that the French warships had destroyed the small band of scruffy Company soldiers for trying to steal their war chest. The men's backgrounds—thieves, cut-throats, villains—provided the Company with a perfect excuse if France accused the English of sending them after the war chest. Spencer need only point to their backgrounds and say that they had obviously been doing some looting for their own personal gain. They all had villainous backgrounds—except Horne, of course.

Spencer was convinced, however, that he would have no need to make excuses to the French government. Instead, his finger would be pointed accusingly at Mauritius, condemning the French for murdering innocent Company employees who had merely been doing their job of protecting Company trading routes.

Spencer did not expect Horne's body to be washed up on shore beneath his window, but he and his fellow Governors were certain that the French would destroy any ship trying to commandeer their precious cargo. The Bombay Marines would be no match for warships; Horne and his men had no hope of survival.

Spencer had set himself a deadline. He planned to wait two months, until the middle of January, and then, when Horne had not returned to Bombay Castle, he would depart for London with the good news—or bad news, as he would report it to the world—of the bloody catastrophe.

Forgetting about Watson and Horne, he thought instead about the way in which he would report the Marines' disappearance—he would call it butchery—in London.

Sitting at his gilt-trimmed table high in Bombay Castle, Spencer imagined himself addressing Parliament, bringing word to the British people about France's merciless slaughter of the Company's little-known, unsung band of work-a-day Marines.

He thought of the prizes he, personally, would receive for his role in this delicate subterfuge to ensure the continuance of war between England and France. A percentage of Company profits? A share of Bombay exports? Would a peerage be too much for him to hope for?

What about Commodore Watson? How would the Company keep Watson's mouth shut? A few bottles of gin should quiet that old blunderbuss.

Commodore Watson arrived back in his own office out of breath and fuming with anger.

Brushing past his secretary, Lieutenant Todwell, he stormed through to the door of the inner chamber.

Lieutenant Todwell followed, gripping a sheaf of papers in his bony white hand. "Sir, I must have a few moments of your time, sir—"

Watson did not pause. "Dash it, not now, Todwell." Slamming the door behind him, he crossed to his desk and collapsed into the chair.

Catching his breath, he dabbed perspiration from his jowls, cursing himself for having accepted this position in the East India Company.

Watson's career in His Majesty's Royal Navy had been distinguished, but he had not shared in rich prize money as had other officers. Consequently, facing retirement with little financial cushioning, he had been lured to India by a fat salary.

The East India Company was rich, and Watson knew that its coffers increased yearly with voyages from England to the Orient and back, bringing home silk, spices, indigo and saltpetre. With profits of three hundred per cent, the East India Company easily won new investors for each outward voyage.

England's East India Company had not been the first European traders to sail to the Orient. The Dutch and Portuguese had led the way, and England, covetously seeing the vast riches transported from India and the East Indian Islands, had quickly begun interfering in the trade routes.

Chartered by Queen Elizabeth in 1600, the Honourable East India Company now—in 1761—surpassed all other European traders. The war with France, over the past five years, had destroyed the French trading company, *Compagnie des Indes Orientales*.

Watson had seen at first hand how important warfare was becoming as part of British trade expansion. Profits were greater with the help of cannons.

Being a military man, he knew that the East India Company had taken an important step forward four years ago, when at Plassey, the former Governor of Bengal, Robert Clive, had led the British Army against Indian troops; in defeating the Nawab of Bengal, he had secured that territory as a monopoly for the Company, and ensured its loyalty by putting a puppet ruler on the throne.

Watson knew, too, that since Plassey, the Company was working more closely with England's War Office and with her Navy Board.

To his frustration, however, the Company did not consider its Bombay Marine a military force—not enough to increase its fighting power. The Marine's small fleet of ships was assigned to safeguard coastlines and draw charts for the captains of Company merchant ships; the Marine's fiercest fighting was against pirates and warring chiefs who threatened trading routes.

In view of this, Watson wondered why Governor Spencer had sent Horne's Marines on such an important and dangerous mission against the French. Was it, as Spencer had said, because Horne had performed so well at Madras? If so, why not secure support for them from the Royal Navy? Or was this new mission like the one to Madras, in that the Navy must not know of it? Weighing the situation, Watson became more frustrated. He realised the limitations of his own power.

What did he have to his credit? Four stone walls of an office; a handsome salary; the prospect of a good pension. There were naval ornaments, too, like his title and his flagship, the *Ferocious*, forty-four guns.

Thinking of the *Ferocious*, he wondered what Spencer would think if he, Watson, sailed to give Horne support at sea. Could he weigh anchor before Spencer was able to stop him?

An idea forming in his brain, Watson pushed back his chair and moved across the room to the map case.

Pulling out maps of the south Indian Ocean, he felt his excitement growing. What was the good of having brave men like Horne if he didn't support them? He should be ready to risk his own life—career and comforts—as Horne did.

His pudgy finger moved down the map from Bombay as he considered where Horne might have sailed from Madagascar in his search for the French treasure ship. Difficult as it was, Watson tried to think like Adam Horne.

20

The *Huma*, the *Tigre* and Oporto

The *Huma*.

The morning sun was at its zenith when Horne's two ships left Oporto's south cove to sail in opposite directions around the small island. Less than an hour earlier, Jingee's foot party had departed on its land manoeuvre.

With Jud as sailing master and Kiro as gun captain aboard the *Huma*, Horne was satisfied that his frigate would be in good command. It was the *Tigre* which worried him.

Through his spyglass, he looked astern, watching Babcock's brig edge the island's southern coastline. The ragged threat of cliffs rose beyond the majestic white pyramid of sails.

Horne doubted if Babcock remembered the reefs as well as he claimed. Groot, too, had most likely over-estimated his powers of memory. But what alternative had there been than to follow the provisional plans and allow the brig to take the southern course? Horne could not confidently exchange places with Babcock and Groot; he remembered fewer details about the reef pattern than they claimed to do. The only other choice would have been to round the island together, following the northern course as a team. But that would have robbed Horne of his one advantage over the French—a double-headed attack.

Watching Babcock disappear to the east, he cursed the fact that circumnavigating the island had become as crucial as seizing the war chest itself. But he had already lost one Marine in battle and could not afford to lose more, whether to gunfire or on reefs.

Kiro spoke behind him. "Larboard gun ports open, sir."

Horne turned to the Japanese gunner. "Keep your men ready and alert, Kiro."

Kiro wore cotton trousers, no shirt or boots, and a red kerchief knotted around his black hair. He did not appear to be troubled that his gun crew consisted of little more than a dozen men.

"I'll give the order to commence firing shortly after we sight the *Calliope*," Horne told him.

"The gun crew's prepared to cross ship, sir," Kiro replied, "and to fire starboard guns at your order."

The *Huma* did not have enough men to fire all thirty-four guns at full strength. Horne depended on Kiro's readiness to move men in shifts. He thought of the strategy as herd tactics, stampeding men rail-to-rail on call. It made the most of minimum manpower.

Dismissing Kiro to stand ready with his skeleton crew, Horne continued pacing the quarterdeck, glum that command of two ships in battle should rest in the hands of only seven men, himself and his six Marines. But hadn't it always been that way? He never had enough officers or crew. But then, he preferred a handful of clever, versatile men to a shipful of dolts.

Glancing back at Babcock's brig now disappearing to the east, he felt the stubble on his chin and remembered he had not shaved all morning. He wore the same soiled breeches he had pulled on with his boots at the first dawn.

A smile widened his lips for the first time that day. He was going into battle no better than some . . . buccaneer.

The *Tigre*

Like Horne aboard the *Huma*, Babcock strode the quarterdeck of the *Tigre*. Studying the brig's braces, watching small, half-naked shapes swinging freely on the yards, he felt white pinpoints of mist spray across the rail, cooling his face and naked chest.

Groot stood at the wheel, blue cap back on his sunbleached hair, and his new Javanese friend, Raji, was up top on the main mast, the two men using their shared understanding of Dutch as communication between mast and helm.

Glancing amidship, Babcock saw that Mustafa had run out the brig's guns, that the bullish Turk stood with his rope garrotte in hand, ready to bellow—or flog—his crew into action. As a precaution, Babcock had assigned Gerard Ury and the rest of the French seaman to the bilge pumps, safely away from the sight of French ships.

Skimming eastward with the wind, Babcock listened to the snap of canvas and felt the deck cant beneath his boots as he raised the spyglass to his eye, looking for some sign of the first reef, a jagged protrusion through the lightly ruffled water.

Seeing no trace of a hidden skerry, he thought back to the map his monkey had eaten.

The island's southern shore had a course of three reefs,

the first being a coral ridge lying half-in, half-out of the water.

He remembered that the map had charted a second reef totally immersed in waves, the rocks lying closer to shore than the first jagged peninsula.

The largest, most perilous reef was the third, a long promontory which formed a craggy extension of the island's northern harbour, a stretch of rocks which itself divided into two further projections jutting east into the Indian Ocean.

Believing that the *Tigre* should soon be approaching the first reef, Babcock bellowed, "Groot, start moving right."

Groot's laughter travelled on the wind; he called, "Babcock, don't you mean . . . starboard?"

Despite the many years Babcock had spent at sea, he could not lose his use of land directions. He thought: The hell with Groot. Let the Dutch cheesehead laugh and call me a lubber. At the end of the day he'll kill himself with his cooking and I'll still be sniffing salt air—left or larboard.

He checked the island's shoreline and saw the craggy coast tapering into a promontory which gradually pushed underwater.

"Groot, first reef coming up—" he thought of the nautical term, "—to larboard."

In Dutch, Groot shouted to Raji; the Javanese sailor's voice echoed high overhead, the command passing around the rigging, the sing-song of the East Indian seamen sounding like a cacophony of strange birds perched in a cage blowing in the wind.

As the *Tigre* slanted towards the sea, responding to Babcock's command, Babcock felt a surge of accomplish-

ment and power; the prow dividing the waves, the brig
cutting obediently away from the first reef.

Cupping both hands to his mouth, he called to Groot,
"Good going, cheesehead."

Groot waved his cap.

Confident of tackling the next reef, Babcock shaded his
eyes against the sun as he tried to remember the second
rocky pattern. It was at that moment he heard a crash from
the bows, a ripping which sounded as if the ship was
being torn apart at the seams.

Oporto.

When Horne's two ships weighed anchor to encircle
Oporto's shoreline from opposite directions, Jingee and the
seven men assigned to him began crossing the island's
dusty plateau on foot. The gangly Asian, Danji, walked at
the head of the column, while Jingee followed at the rear,
shouting in Hindi for the men to trot in neat formation.

Seamen from the Malabar coast; Malagasy fishermen
recruited from Port Diego-Suarez; pirates captured off the
pattimar—Jingee's group was an odd assortment of men,
some wearing turbans wrapped around their heads, others
having rags knotted at four corners for protection against
the sun.

Nearing the centre of Oporto, Jingee shrilled for Danji
to veer the men around the island's rocky spine. Calling
their first break, he allowed them one short gulp from the
waterskin.

At a patch of scrub pine, he noticed that the men were
becoming relaxed in their discipline, that they were beginning to laugh and talk among themselves.

He ordered, "A man who has wind enough to talk, has
wing enough to . . . run."

Jogging beside the bare-legged seamen, he ran them at a brisk pace, remembering his training on Bull Island earlier in the year to become one of Horne's special Bombay Marines. Those days seemed years ago.

Reaching the ravine where he had hidden the Frenchman's body, Jingee fell to the rear of the column. Noting the unobtrusive mound of earth and twigs, he returned satisfied to his place beside the puffing seamen, counting, "One, two, three, four . . . one, two, three, four . . ."

Tall brown grass appeared on the horizon, and Jingee knew they had already come to the island's northern cliffs. He raised his hand to slow the men, not wanting them to stir the dust and betray their arrival to the French ships below in the cove.

Moving to the front of the column, he approached the precipice and glanced over the cliffs.

Below, he saw that the French crew no longer lounged on the sandy white shore. Instead, small boats were returning them to the *Calliope*, and the brig was making preparations to weigh anchor. He wondered if anyone had noticed yet that two Marines were missing.

Near the eastern edge of the cove's mouth, a rowing-boat passed from the brig to the frigate which Jingee was certain had come from Mauritius. The small open boat was carrying officers' credentials, he guessed, and messages from Captain Le Clerc for French headquarters. Studying both vessels, he saw no sign of the war chest but he was sure it was there.

Beckoning the men to move forward to the edge of the cliff, Jingee mimed with the palms of his hands for them to fall to the ground to avoid being spotted from below. Danji pushed down those who did not understand Jingee's orders.

Jingee lay in the middle of the seven men, pointing down to the *Calliope*.

He whispered, "Gold."

Danji translated the word; whispers passed up and down the line.

Jingee picked up a rock and mimed throwing it over the cliff.

Turbans and knotted handkerchiefs nodded, knowing laughs running along the row of seamen.

Jingee asked Danji if any man had a question.

Danji pointed to himself. "There are so few of us, and so many of them. What good will it do throwing a rock or two at such big ships?" Danji gestured to the French vessels.

Jingee pointed north; he pointed south; he explained, "Captain Horne and Babcock. They're coming this way on their ships. We shall throw rocks when we see them firing at the French. We shall also roll trees to make landslides. We shall run back and forth to raise clouds of dust. The French down there will look up here and think an army has come to descend on them."

"Ahhh." Danji nodded and explained the plan to the men.

At the far end of the line, a flat-faced boy with a turban pulled down over his ears raised his hand.

Jingee called for him to speak; the boy went on wagging his hand and Jingee soon saw that, instead of wanting to ask a question, he was pointing towards the cove's shoreline.

Looking below the cliffs, Jingee saw four men from the *Calliope* climbing the incline, muskets slung over their shoulders. They were coming to look for the patrolmen he had killed. Jingee was certain of it.

21

The Second Reef

The *Tigre*.

Babcock hurtled down the quarterdeck ladder, taking four rungs at a time. Crossing the gangway, he leaped over the forecastle, hurrying to the bows to inspect what had caused the crashing timber.

The ripping sound had ceased and the brig was sailing soundlessly through the slightly-lapping water, but Babcock feared they had entered the second reef before he and Groot had suspected they would. The *Tigre* had struck uncharted boulders and he was worried that they might encounter more.

He called to Mustafa, "Send a boy below to check for damage."

Hearing Groot shouting, Babcock looked over his shoulder and saw the Dutchman frantically waving his blue cap, pointing across the bows.

Gripping tightly to avoid falling overboard, Babcock peered down into the water. He saw long strands of weed trailing into the translucent depths, with shapes of oddly-striped fish swimming unafraid near the surface. But there was no sign of underwater snares, no submerged ridges, no continuation of a reef pattern.

Looking back at Groot, Babcock was surprised to see him still pointing, bewildered to hear him shouting, "Reef . . ."

Confused, he turned back to the surf.

This time, he noticed that the sea bed was shoaling quickly. He looked farther out to sea and saw what Groot was pointing at.

Jagged shapes lay beneath the water's ruffled surface.

They must be approaching shoals from the second reef sooner than he had anticipated; Babcock waved his hand, signalling Groot to steer to starboard.

Groot was already spinning the wheel and shouting to Raji overhead in the rigging; a chorus of voices spread through the masts and spars as canvas snapped and lines groaned.

Feeling the brig slope from the coastline, Babcock kept his eyes on the pattern of sharply-toothed reefs, waiting to hear a crack at any moment. He heard only the slap of the waves, the brig cutting forward on its eastward tack.

Leaning over the rails, he saw sharp boulders only a few feet away from the hull, the brig gliding between a range of submerged peaks.

He tried to remember the chart, recalling patterns in the shape of a "T," a channel which ran perpendicularly between the first and second reef. Believing they were approaching the T's crossarm, he waved for Groot to move in a straight line out to sea.

The *Tigre* remained angled to the coastline.

Frustrated, Babcock looked over his shoulder to see why Groot was disobeying the order. The Dutchman

Groot stood stalwart at the wheel, stubbornly shaking his head.

Babcock boomed, "What the hell's the matter, you cheesehead?" He was angry. Wasn't this ship under his command? Would he have to discipline Groot for insubordination?

Groot nodded in the direction in which Babcock had pointed.

Babcock ran along the gangway, looking into the water. He finally saw what Groot had meant—an underwater rock formation like a tabletop, a shallow flatness extending at least twelve feet wide and probably thirty feet in length.

Wiping beads of perspiration from his forehead, he could only feel relief at Groot's stubbornness. The *Tigre* would have scraped bottom, wrecking her hull.

More cautious as he proceeded towards the third reef, Babcock remembered that Horne had given strict orders for the *Tigre* not to sail too far out to sea after clearing the third reef and so risk being spotted too soon by the French frigate which might be anchored at the cove's mouth. Horne wanted Babcock's brig in a clear position to lead the enemy frigate to sea, clearing the cove's mouth so that Horne could sail into the cove and attack the *Calliope*.

As they moved towards the third reef, he checked to see that Groot was gaining sea room.

Groot's face still glowered from their near miss.

Uncaring that the Dutchman might be angry—or had even lost trust in him—Babcock leaned back over the railing and looked down into the ruffled water.

Seeing nothing, he guessed that if they kept to sea, they would escape the last reef.

"Starboard," he waved, motioning Groot seaward.

The slant of the ship told Babcock that Groot was following orders. Good. He was pleased that they agreed on their recollection of the reef pattern, and glad that he would not have to kick Groot's butt for insubordination.

Off the pocked shoreline, a saw-toothed range rose above the water, convincing Babcock that they were passing—escaping—the third reef.

His spirits lifted; the nightmare was coming to an end; he could concentrate now on the enemy.

Groot shouted from the wheel.

Wondering if Groot was becoming temperamental, perhaps even smug over his good performance, Babcock wearily raised his eyes to see what the trouble was this time.

A frigate lay directly in front of them.

"Sail ho!" called a voice from the mast.

Leaping to his feet, Babcock shouted, "Bloody hell. The frogs." He had been concentrating so hard on the reefs that he had forgotten about watching for the point when they would round the island's southeastern tip.

"Mustafa," he ordered, "prepare those bloody guns."

The mainmast hailed, "Signal flag, ahoy."

The French recognised the *Tigre* as one of their ships. Horne had prepared Babcock for such an event. He had also advised the American not to waste time by simulating fraudulent flag calls.

Turning, Babcock boomed, "I got a message for those frogs."

To Mustafa, he shouted, "Grape on top of round shot."

Mustafa, rope garrotte in hand, cursed the men into action.

Babcock called to the helm, "Swing around this bloody tub, Groot, and give me a good aim at that bleeding frigate."

He felt himself gaining more confidence. There was nothing like a good fight to get a man's blood up.

Behind him, a voice reported, "Water coming through the hull, sir."

Babcock turned, remembering the Asian boy whom Mustafa had sent to check the damage caused by the rock scrape.

"How serious is it?" he asked.

The boy wore only a *dhoti*, and his face was smudged with soot. "The French sailors down there are keeping it out with the bilge pumps."

"Good." Babcock nodded. "That'll keep them busy and out of trouble."

He turned back to the frigate, feeling as if the situation was in his favour.

The *Tigre* tacked, parading her gunports to the French frigate; the guns boomed, shaking the deck, enveloping the brig with smoke.

As the black cloud lifted in the wind, Babcock looked toward the enemy and saw that Mustafa had scored a broadside without firing a ranging shot.

"You did it, Ugly," he shouted. "You did it. You got 'em right in the belly."

Mustafa grinned, snapping the rope between his clenched fists.

Determined to score a succession of three strikes before leading the frigate to sea, Babcock ordered, "Go for her a second time. Get her right in the guts like last time."

The cords stood out on Mustafa's neck as he shouted at his gunners, swinging his garrotte in the air; the cannons exploded, making the brig's board chatter and the men fall back from the thunder.

Babcock was euphoric. "Look. Those frogs are smoking like a tuppenny pipe."

With one last strike to score before heading seaward, Babcock looked to the wheel. He was surprised to see Groot labouring the spokes; glancing overhead, he saw the brig in a tack.

He muttered: What the hell? Why's Groot moving so early?

"You idiot," Babcock shouted at Groot. "You're ruining our third broadside, you cheesehead."

Groot's eyes remained on the rigging, his hands spinning the wheel.

Ready to explode at Groot for such cavalier behaviour, Babcock looked back across the bows.

To landward, waves lapped a long, rocky spur.

Babcock felt his legs go limp. Damn it to hell. Groot was right again.

The third reef clawed into two formations, fingers which thrust from the cove's mouth into the Indian ocean. In his jubilation, Babcock had forgotten.

It was pitch-black down in the hold of the *Tigre*, the flames in all lamps aboard ship having been extinguished at the outset of battle.

Water rose from the reef snag in the hull, the bilge pumps no longer able to keep out the flood as the guns roared overhead.

Gerard Ury squatted on a bench, his calloused hands working a wooden pump as he listened to the other French seamen around him anxiously discussing the battle.

"I say—let's mutiny," one argued in French.

"Don't be stupid. We're outnumbered five to one."

"It doesn't matter," said a third voice in the darkness. "Who do you think this ship's fighting? One of *our* ships, that's who. French. I say mutiny and help put a quick end to it."

A Marseilles accent cut through the clank of the pump in the darkness. "How do you know it's French? If these men are pirates as I think they are, then they could be fighting a British ship. If we mutiny, we'll be helping to put ourselves in the hands of King George."

Ury liked the idea of mutiny, if for no other reason than to get out of the humid, wet darkness.

He volunteered, "I'll go and see."

The voice next to him said, "When you get on deck, Ury, the first thing you should do is look for the flag on the enemy ship."

Another man offered, "Then look to see if we can attack these pirate scum."

"But beware," cautioned the voice from Marseilles. "There might be a guard on the hatch."

"If there is, I'll say the flood's worse," suggested Ury. "That water's pouring in faster. That these old pumps can't cope."

"Good. That should panic them."

"Good luck," whispered the men. "God be with you."

Ury felt his way in the darkness, keeping his head low as his bare feet sloshed through the water.

Gripping the ladder, he climbed carefully up, up, up the slimy rungs. The ladder shuddered as another strike bombarded the brig; Ury paused, waiting for the ladder to steady.

An overhead glint of daylight caught his eye and he resumed climbing, his heart beating in excitement. What flag would he see flying across the waves—England or France?

22

Ambush

Oporto.

Jingee divided the seven Asian seamen of his land patrol into two groups. Danji took three men towards the top of a hill while Jingee led the remaining men further down the same incline. Jingee had chosen the section of the island's slope where he suspected the four French Marines off the *Calliope* would climb to the island's plateau. He was more convinced than ever that they had come in search of the two men he had killed.

Hiding behind the boulders with his men, he waited for the French troops to trudge nearer, wondering if Danji and the other Asians were trustworthy. Would they give away their positions when the French troops drew closer? Did they have more loyalty to France than to England? So many East Indians hated the growing might of the British.

Looking up the slope, Jingee saw no sign of Danji or his four men. He could only see the long narrow mound of earth covering the rope which Danji had laid across the path of the Frenchmen. The rope had been Danji's idea.

Jingee had only thought of ambushing from behind boulders. So perhaps Danji was trustworthy. What about the others?

Looking back to the four French troops, he saw that they were climbing steadily closer; he could hear their voices but was unable to understand what they were saying.

The day was hot, and one of the four troops had taken off his tall blue hat; he was little more than a boy. The other three all had moustaches, but none was older than Jingee himself; their white teeth flashed against their sunburnt skin as they laughed.

Jingee forced down a rush of guilt, trying not to think of the young men having families at home, sweethearts waiting for them to return, dreams for the future.

He kept reminding himself: It's their life or mine. They'll find their friends dead and won't leave the island until they learn who killed them.

Glancing back at his own men, Jingee saw that they were well hidden behind the boulders. So far nobody was betraying him.

As the French troops began passing directly in front of him, sabres and muskets clanking, Jingee held his breath.

The rancid smell from their bodies travelled on the breeze. Jingee wrinkled his nose, raising his head to watch the four young men climb towards Danji's hideout. As they approached the rope hidden across their path, his hand tightened on the handle of his dagger. Rising from his knees, he beckoned his men to follow.

He gave the dove call, the gentle coo . . . coo . . . coo.

The four Frenchmen kept on climbing, laughing, unsuspecting.

Up the hill, Danji and his three men sprang from their

hiding places—two men pulling opposite ends of the rope—and ran down the incline, the rope stretched between them, acting as a scythe to cut down the Frenchmen.

The young troops fell backwards, muskets and sabres clattering to the ground, and Jingee whistled his men to attack from behind their rocks.

Wielding knives and stones, the Asians sprang to their feet and fell upon the toppled Frenchmen, stabbing with their knife blades and aiming sharp blows with the stones they clutched in their hands.

Danji's men joined in the massacre, the four Asians gripping a stone in each hand, pummelling the young soldiers on their heads, chests and backs.

When the four Frenchmen were silenced, their blood-covered bodies motionless in the sun, Danji organised their burial while Jingee hurried to look over the ridge.

To seaward, he saw Babcock's *Tigre* leading the Mauritius frigate to sea, leaving the *Calliope* unprotected in the cove.

Looking northward, he smiled as he saw Horne sweeping down in the *Huma*, sailing towards the cove's mouth.

Everything was going to plan.

Looking around him for the trees and dried stumps he had noticed earlier, he knew that it was time for him and his seamen to move on to the next stage of their land manoeuvre.

23

The *Calliope*

The *Huma*.

Adam Horne stood to windward on the quarterdeck of the *Huma*, spyglass directed south, studying the gunfire from the *Tigre* booming towards the frigate which flew the French colours. He was relieved to see the *Tigre* tack after venturing perilously close to the finger of the third reef. Had Babcock and Groot forgotten the last obstacle? The rocks were not visible through Horne's spyglass but he remembered enough of the destroyed chart to know that Babcock had reached that perilous position.

A roar from the French frigate's guns told Horne a fight was underway, that Babcock's challenge had been accepted by the enemy. Judging from the size of the three-masted vessel, he feared that Babcock might be outmatched.

Telling himself he must concentrate on the challenge waiting for the *Huma*, he turned his spyglass to the cove, where the *Calliope* was anchored off the sandy shore. Jingee's information had been correct. Horne only hoped that the transfer had not yet taken place, that the war chest was still aboard the small brig.

His mind on Jingee, he raised his glass up the tall cliffs backing the shoreline. The barren plateau showed no sign of life, the skyline broken only by a few shapes of trees—certainly not suspicious from the enemy's vantage point.

Horne turned his attention back to his own plan of attack.

As the *Huma* passed through the north cove's wide mouth, Horne studied the trim lines of the *Calliope*, remembering that stormy morning when she had escaped him, abandoning a skeleton crew on the *Tigre* to fend for themselves.

Stuffing the spyglass into his waistband, he held both hands to his mouth, ordering, "Set course northwest."

Jud stood tall at the wheel, his mahogany-brown face a blend of determination and amusement, moving his lips as if he were talking to some invisible companion.

Horne turned his head, calling, "Mind the jib."

A map showed the north cove to be a deep-water harbour, but Horne saw from the cliffs and snug shoreline that manoeuvrability would be tight if the *Calliope* gave him a battle. He must not fool himself about the available sea room which would be further reduced by the wind force cutting down from the surrounding plateau.

"Jud, firm towards the southern shore; those cliffs there."

"Aye, aye, sir."

As the frigate slid windward of the brig, Kiro reminded him, "Sir, larboard guns ready."

Horne gauged the approach; as the brig drew closer, he

decided to begin the peppering of grapeshot, foregoing the usual ranging shot.

Hands cupped to his mouth, he ordered, "Prepare larboard guns to fire . . ."

Horne studied the brig through the spyglass; he was close enough to see the pandemonium aboard the enemy ship, the French crew frenzied by the sudden appearance of the *Huma* in the cove. Their surprise, he hoped, would be incapacitating.

Did the *Calliope* recognise the *Huma* from their last encounter? Was Captain Le Clerc aboard with the crew members he had taken from the *Tigre*? If so, what identity was he assigning to Horne's ragged band of men in the pirate ship? Did Le Clerc have any clue that they were after the war chest? Had he guessed by now that this attack had been carefully orchestrated to catch him unawares, unprotected?

Another question which preoccupied Horne was whether or not Captain Le Clerc had spotted that it was his former ship, the *Tigre*, leading the French frigate from the cove's mouth. Le Clerc would enjoy a clear view across the natural harbour to where Babcock was at work.

The *Calliope* had weighed anchor and was opening her gunports as she caught the wind. Horne abandoned his musing to gauge his position before calling orders to fire. Through his spyglass he saw the French topsails blossom like a flower.

Another pattern of whiteness attracted his attention: a puff of smoke from the gunports. Then came a splash between him and the brig. Had Le Clerc fired a ranging shot? Or had he lost his composure and fired too soon?

Reminding himself that waiting was the most important element of battle, Horne felt the *Huma* tilt on her course across the cove, lining to give a clear range for the cannon.

The moment to fire was coming closer and, his heart beating faster, Horne shouted, "Prepare to fire and . . ."

The moment must be right or all was wasted. Each second was an hour. But each wasted shot was an invitation to defeat.

". . . Fire!"

The *Huma* trembled from the explosion.

"Stand by to go about," shouted Horne through the smoke cloud.

He called to Jud, "Head to the wind."

"Aye, aye, sir," answered the bass voice through the scattering cloud.

Kiro reported from larboard, "Gun crew prepared for orders, sir."

Horne risked, "Men to starboard."

Pleased, he listened to the rush of bare feet across deck; he knew Kiro had had no time to have the deck sanded to avoid slipping.

Had he ever conducted a battle so makeshift? Horne forgot about his improvisations as the *Huma* caught the wind, lying over no more than a few degrees. With an exhilarating lurch, the shrouds sighed, yards shivered from the quick tug and stress.

As the topsails bellied against the plateau wind, Horne saw the French brig catching the breeze, tacking southeast, bringing her head to the wind as she set a course straight for the *Huma*.

"Set course for northeast," he called to Jud.

"Aye, aye, sir."

"The wind's more powerful than you think," cautioned Horne, eyes on the cove's northern perimeter.

"Aye, aye, Captain."

Horne gauged the point inside the cove at which the two ships would pass. "Tops'll short."

The enemy brig, closing the gap between herself and Horne, fired another ball.

The enemy was as out of range on the new tack as they had been from the anchorage. Horne wondered how nervous Captain Le Clerc was.

"Steer firm, Jud."

"Aye, aye, sir."

Two cables distant, Horne studied the French ship on her course to pass abeam the *Huma*. The space between the two ships was shortening as they continued on a parallel course, their prows closing.

Raising his hand to Kiro, Horne shouted, "Prepare guns to fire and . . ." He waited. ". . . Fire."

Kiro's cannons belched flames, blue clouds of smoke rising in thick puffs.

Feeling the deck tremble, Horne heard timbers crash, sails rip, the screams of men pierce the air.

The two ships continued past one another, timbers groaning, smoke spreading in their wake.

Realising for the first time that sweat was pouring from his brow, that he was burning with body heat, Horne pulled off his shirt. Towelling his face with the garment, he shouted, "Stand by to go about."

The men needed no urging.

The spokes of the wheel spun through Jud's hands; the topmen were ready to head into the wind, sails thundering, canvas snapping. The activity aloft was matched by Kiro stampeding his crew back to the larboard guns.

The *Huma*, catching her stays, did not move quickly

enough for Horne's liking, and he bellowed, "Hang her up in that wind, men."

Listening to the ropes scream, blocks groan, water creaming in the frigate's wake, Horne realised how lucky he was to have the few good men he had. But he knew he could not push them so hard for long.

Kiro reported, "Larboard guns sponged and loaded, sir."

"Canister on round shot?"

"Aye, aye, sir."

Horne saw Le Clerc's brig tacking, preparing to return for the *Huma*.

At the moment when an idea began forming in his mind, Jud shouted, "Captain, look ashore. Above the brig's position."

Horne raised his eyes and, there on the cove's southern plateau, he saw a cloud of dust rise along the rim, the cloud becoming stronger as—yes, it looked like an army storming down the incline to the harbour.

Jingee was doing his job. Was it making Le Clerc hesitate?

Snapping open his spyglass, Horne looked to see how Babcock was faring with the enemy frigate outside the cove. Before proceeding with his strategy for the *Huma*, he must know the exact progress of all the Marines—inside the cove, outside it and above on the ridge.

24

Above the Cove

Oporto.

There had been an unforeseen problem among the men of Jingee's land patrol before they began pushing the boulders and logs down the cliff.

After burying the four young French Marines, Jingee had ordered his patrol to begin the next step of their manoeuvre. But the seamen hesitated near the scene of the carnage, a few men sinking to their haunches, unable to walk. Two held their stomachs, bodies doubled over, spewing sickness onto the ground, while one lay face down on the ground.

Jingee's deputy, Danji, shook his head resignedly and raised both hands to the sun, blaming the heat for the men's suddenly uncooperative conduct.

Jingee knew better. It was not the heat. All the men were seamen; all were used to sun beating down on them. No, they were squeamish from the bloody atrocity they had committed, and from the sight of the dead bodies of the French Marines.

Running to the first man, Jingee grabbed him by the ear, shouting, "There's more work to do."

The man stared at him, shaking his head.

Jingee turned and looked out beyond the edge of the plateau. Below him, he could see two battles progressing: one confrontation inside the cove, between Horne and the *Calliope*; the other outside the cove, cannon fire booming between Babcock's brig and the frigate from Mauritius.

Knowing that the Captain sahib was depending on him to create a diversion, Jingee turned back to the reluctant seaman and slapped him across the face; he slapped him a second time, harder than the first, and shoved him towards the precipice.

Grabbing another man, he saw his mouth gaping with horror and, pulling back his hand, slapped him smartly across the face.

The man held his cheek in astonishment, staring disbelievingly at Jingee.

Jingee hissed, "If you don't start pushing those rocks as I told you to, I'll shove *you* down the cliff."

The man hesitated, shaking his head.

Jingee gripped him firmly by the neck and pulled him kicking and screaming to the edge of the cliff.

"No, no," pleaded the young man. "I obey you. I do what you say."

Jingee boxed him sharply on the ear, gave him a kick in the *dhoti* and shoved him after the first man.

Turning, he looked challengingly at the others.

Quickly, the men lowered their eyes and hurried to the plateau's edge, taking their places obediently behind logs and boulders.

Taking up his position at the cliff's edge, Jingee chopped down his arm through the air, ordering, *"Heave . . . heave . . ."* He believed the problem had been settled.

25

Outside the Cove

The *Tigre*.

Outside the cove, cannon fire from the French frigate jolted Babcock back to his senses.

He had come close—too damned close—to losing the *Tigre* on the hidden finger of the last reef. He knew he could make no more foolish mistakes like that. It was reassuring, however, to know that he had finally cleared all the reefs. He would remember the location of that last rocky prong and stay well away from there.

The important thing, he told himself, was that he had lured the French frigate out to sea. He had cleared the path for Horne to sail into the cove and bear down on the treasure ship.

Standing in the *Tigre*'s prow, Babcock took stock of the situation to decide what he should do next.

His brig stood between the cove and the French frigate to the east. Inside the cove, cannon fire was being exchanged between Horne and the treasure ship. They had obviously gone into battle.

Babcock suspected, too, that Jingee had begun the land diversion from the cliffs. Would Jingee's patrol seriously disturb the enemy as Horne had predicted? Babcock didn't know.

Looking at the French frigate beyond the brig's prow, he told himself, "That frog captain out there can hear the cannon fire from inside the cove, too. He wants to move in to give assistance to that little ship with all that gold on it. The only thing standing in his way is me.

"So what would I do if I was that frog captain from Mauritius and I wanted to save that bloody war chest from being captured by some strangers?"

He stood for a moment, studying the three-masted enemy ship. "That frog is coming back to try to smash me to kindling wood," he told himself. "That's what he's going to try to do. He can probably do it, too. Then, with me out of the way, he's going into the cove to help pound Horne down to the bottom of the sea."

What was he to do?

Babcock knew his own gunpower. Mustafa's seven cannon run out could provide little more than a nuisance. So how could he continue stalling the enemy outside the cove while Horne moved in on the war chest? He could bluff. He could dally. But the few men he had were tired and becoming weak.

And what about the French seamen down in the bilges? Would they rally in support of their fellow countrymen when they heard cannon fire?

Babcock looked back to the jagged perimeter of the cove. Remembering how he had almost struck the last hidden reef, he had an inspiration. There was one way he could smash the enemy frigate to bits.

It would be risky. It would require Groot's full co-operation. The Dutchman would have to understand fully what sailing manoeuvres Babcock intended and there must be no confusion between them about nautical and land talk—starboard and larboard, this way and that.

An explosion shook the *Tigre*.

Hitting the deck, Babcock felt the timbers shudder beneath his spreadeagled body; splinters and smoke flew around him; a wave swept over the bulwark, water crashing through the smoke from the broadside.

Time was running out. Babcock knew he had to take that crazy chance or they would all end up on the bottom of the Indian Ocean.

Raising himself to his hands and knees in the dense smoke, Babcock looked around him to gauge the broadside's destruction. Through the slap of waves and agonised groans, he heard Mustafa's gruff voice bellowing at the crew to charge the cannon.

Babcock rose unsteadily to his feet and stumbled forward. Tripping over a bundle of rags, he looked down at his feet and saw that it was a dead body. It was Ury, the French helmsman's mate. What had Ury been doing out of the bilges? Poor wretch. Well, he was dead, and now Babcock saw other bodies in the black smoke.

Having no medicine for the wounded, no time to move the dead, he shouted through the smoke drift, "Give 'em hell, boys! Give 'em hell!"

Dark shapes moved along the gunports; Babcock saw Mustafa bent over the cannon butt; he heard him shouting to the two remaining gunmen as a fuse glittered in the dusty light.

Babcock urged, "Blow 'em to Kingdom Come, you ugly old Turk. Blow 'em to—"

Another strike bombarded the little brig. Babcock fell backwards, hitting his shoulder on the coaming; the deck lurched beneath his sprawled body and, for a fleeting moment, he could not see through a cloud of black smoke.

Cursing to himself, he grabbed the gangway, his eyes burning from the smoke as he heard a new wave of cries rising from the gunport.

Another lashing like that, he told himself, and this little tub will be gone for good.

Groping his way through the confusion towards the helm, Babcock repeated to himself, "Get to Groot . . . Get to Groot . . . Convince the old cheesehead that your plan's not all that crazy . . . Convince him that it's the only way we can keep those French bastards from turning us into frog soup."

Another blast sent him flying, his head striking the mast.

Mustafa's memories were of a sunbaked house. There were goats pegged to the earth floor and grandparents sitting on the flat roof drying tomatoes in the sun. The vision was of Alanya, the Turkish village where young girls weaved cloth with their mothers, young boys mended fishnets with the old men, and where Mustafa had always been unhappy, always fighting with his brothers.

His next vision was of a dark, crowded prison. The cells were honeycombed beneath Bombay Castle. He had been a prisoner there less than a year ago.

Lying face down on the deck of the *Tigre*, Mustafa remembered how Captain Horne had chosen him from that prison to be a Bombay Marine, how Horne had taken him to Bull Island to train him to fight like a man, not like an animal.

Death and confusion surrounded him on deck. He knew that the Marines were losing their battle, but he could not gather the strength to continue fighting, to help Horne, to help Groot and Kiro and Jingee and Jud and . . . yes . . . even to help Babcock.

Tasting the blood that filled his mouth, Mustafa became angry with himself. For the first time in his life he wanted to help someone, and he couldn't.

His eyesight was dimming. Mustafa smiled. It was a good feeling to want to help someone. Despite the pain cutting through his chest, the total numbness in both legs, he felt a strange inner glow.

It was funny, wasn't it, he thought, that he should be happy only now, when he was dying?

So maybe his wandering life hadn't been totally wasted. He was knowing this little bit of happiness; he had had these few months as one of Horne's Marines; he at last had some friends.

Mustafa died, smiling.

26

Inside the Cove

The *Huma*.

Through his spyglass Horne saw Le Clerc's brig catching the wind at the back of the cove, approaching the *Huma* again, as a large dust cloud rose from the cliffs behind the French vessel.

What did Le Clerc make of Jingee's landslide? Had it disconcerted him as Horne hoped? Did Le Clerc think it could be an armed patrol? Land reinforcement?

Watching the French brig bear down on him, he proceeded with his own plan of attack.

Le Clerc was obviously going to sweep alongside the *Huma* and fire a close-range broadside to wreak the maximum destruction.

Instead of widening the distance between the two ships, Horne decided to decrease it to give the French captain a surprise.

To Kiro he called, "Seize grappling hooks."

Kiro pulled the red kerchief from around his head and,

using it to wipe the soot from his face, smiled at Horne's order.

Horne approached Kiro's soiled, tattered crew. "Men, we're going to board the enemy ship."

Enough of the Malagasy fishermen and Indian pirates understood Horne's English to explain it to the others, and excitement spread through the odd assortment of men.

Horne's voice was stern. "You will arm yourselves with pistols from amidship. Use anything at hand if there aren't enough pistols—knives, axes, clubs."

Enthusiastically, the men turned to begin a weapon search.

"Stop." Horne raised his hands. "I'm not ordering a blood bath. Remember that. I'm sending you to capture an enemy ship, not to lay waste. You are to fight to protect yourselves, but any man I see killing without reason will hang from the yard till he's dead."

He singled out from the crew a turbaned man whom he had observed translating his speech to the others. "Explain to each man exactly what I said."

To Kiro, he ordered, "Station your men along the larboard rail with their grappling lines."

The Japanese gunman's grin vanished.

"When you secure us to the enemy ship," explained Horne, "I'll board the rest of the men from midship."

Kiro raised his eyes to the rigging.

Horne pointed. "You board your men fore."

There were less than fifty men aboard the *Huma*; Horne had their whole attention as the ship progressed towards the *Calliope*, sailing under shortened topsail from the back of the cove. The plateau wind cracked the canvas in loud snaps but the cove's waves were low, little more than neat rows of whitecaps.

To the helm, Horne shouted, "Jud, you and ten men shall remain aboard ship."

The African's voice boomed, "Aye, aye, sir."

"You are to protect the *Huma* as the rest of us go to take the *Calliope*."

Glancing over his shoulder at the enemy's approaching sails, Horne ordered, "Now seize those grappling lines, Kiro, and make your men put their muscle into their throw."

As the band of seamen ran into action, Horne leaped to the railing and pulled the spyglass from his waistband to observe any change in the enemy's activity.

Looking through the lens, he smiled as he saw Le Clerc's crew abandoning their gun ports. The French had spotted the *Huma*'s crew forming boarding parties; they were responding in turmoil.

Anxious to board the *Calliope* before Le Clerc had time to organise his crew to repel boarders, Horne made a quick check of his subordinates.

Jud stood at the wheel; Kiro and his crew crowded the railings, armed with a variety of weapons and holding the grappling lines ready to hurl; the top hands were rapidly descending ratlines and shrouds to join Horne's boarding party, some men already arming themselves with knives, or any makeshift weapons they could find—iron, wood, rope.

Looking beyond the French brig to the island's shore, Horne sighted his spyglass on Jingee's patrol climbing onto logs, some of the patrol men already paddling towards the two ships. Horne had discussed a boarding party with Jingee this morning, planning how the land patrol could join the men from the frigate in hand-to-hand combat. He looked around for a tarred rope to drop for Jingee to climb from the water.

Spyglass stowed in the companionway, tarred rope in

hand, Horne felt the wind against his cheek as he studied the prows of the two ships approaching one another.

At last he heard the collision of timber, felt the *Huma* shake, and called, "Throw grappling hooks."

Six spiked iron hooks flew from the *Huma*; four caught onto the *Calliope* and Kiro shouted to the men to pull the fastened lines as the other hooks were rethrown.

Horne waved his men forward; Kiro's crew followed from the bow.

Amid whoops and cries, Horne boarded the *Calliope*, pausing only to tie one end of his tarred rope to the starboard rail, dropping the other end overboard for Jingee's patrol to climb from their makeshift boats.

As he stood up, he spotted a swarthy man lunging towards him, levelling a sword at his chest.

Dodging the stab, Horne pulled the knife from his waistband and slashed for the man's weapon arm, grabbing the sword as it fell. He swung the brass and silver hilt against the attacker's chin, knocking him over the rail. Then he leaped down onto the deck, looking for someone who might be Le Clerc. He was determined to make the French captain surrender and save unnecessary bloodshed.

Seeing three men rushing towards him, he dodged towards the mast, raising the sword to stab at the first, a man gripping a flintlock.

Kiro jumped from the forecastle, landing on the other two men. Kicking one man in the chest, he chopped his hand against the other's head.

As Kiro used his ancient *Karate* to fell the two seamen, Horne stabbed the third attacker's pistol hand. The weapon clattered to deck and Horne kicked it towards the scuppers, raising his eyes in time to see a fourth man running towards Kiro with a blade.

Kiro also saw the knifeman; he bent forward, flinging the man over his shoulder and sending him down onto the deck with a loud crack.

Horne brought his boot down on the man's hand; the blade fell from his grasp.

Scooping up the knife from deck, Horne tossed it to Kiro and turned towards the fighting raging behind him.

Metal clanked; fists flew; flintlocks popped here and there in the clash. In the midst of the fighting, Horne saw that Jingee and his men had boarded the ship and joined in the combat, wielding rocks, flailing ropes knotted with iron spikes.

Horne could still see no officer in uniform, no man distinctly different from the fighting Lascars and other Asian seamen. He hoped Le Clerc had not taken the war chest and abandoned ship as he had done once before; perhaps he had escaped on the frigate which Babcock was battling outside the cove.

At that moment, he heard a crashing sound to seaward. As he turned, his first thought was that Babcock had again forgotten the reef and had gone aground on the third rocky finger which pronged out into the Indian Ocean.

The sight that greeted Horne beyond the cove was shocking but, at the same time, strangely awe-inspiring.

For no reason which was immediately apparent, he saw the French frigate's mainmast crash fore, knocking her foremast towards her prow, tearing her mizzenmast in its wake, jerking riggings, ripping sails, making yards twist and fly and shatter in sudden confusion. It took Horne a few moments to realise that the French ship from Mauritius had struck the hidden reef.

The terrible destruction went on, holding him transfixed.

The wind off the sea flipped the hull aft to fore, smashing it with a mighty force down against the rocks, scattering cannon and spars and men's bodies—everything—in all directions like weightless specks of sand.

A chill of horror crept up Horne's spine as he watched the surf roll the tangled ship towards the shoreline, revolving its hull, dragging booms, water creaming in the snarled confusion.

Regaining his senses, Horne remembered the *Tigre*. Were his men also in danger?

He sighed with relief as the Marine brig sailed northeast from the reef; the little ship looked ragged from cannon fire but she was safe.

Turning back to the disaster at the mouth of the cove, Horne saw the surf thrash the wrecked frigate against the rocky shoreline, the wind and waves hammering destruction.

Was it an accident, this horror?

Horne answered the question for himself.

No.

He knew intuitively that Babcock and Groot had lured the French ship onto the hidden rocks; it had probably been the one way they had had to overcome such a heavily-armed ship.

Feeling himself break into a victorious smile, Horne was suddenly ashamed of his pleasure.

But what a victory it was.

The cannon had quieted on his own ship as well as aboard Le Clerc's *Calliope*. The wrecked frigate continued to hold every man's rapt attention, bringing battle to a shocking end, both outside—and inside—the cove.

27

All that Glitters

Commodore Watson stood beside Adam Horne at the foot of Mustafa's freshly dug grave. Horne's five Marines waited, heads reverently bowed, a few yards down the slope—Babcock, Groot, Jingee, Jud, Kiro.

Watson held his gold-braided cocked hat in one hand, mopping a handkerchief around his fleshy neck with the other hand, perspiring profusely in Oporto's morning heat.

He asked, "How many men did you bury, Horne?"

"We dug fourteen graves, sir."

Watson glanced at the rocky earth. "No easy work in this soil."

"I put it to the men's vote, sir. They felt that graves would be more fitting than sea burials. Many of the dead, sir, had been pressed into service against their will."

"I don't know if I would have been so considerate as to let my men vote on such a matter." Watson fanned his hat, glancing at the neat line of burial plots above him on the slope. "It's hard work burying fourteen men in this terrain."

"There were more than fourteen casualties, sir. But we only dug fourteen graves."

Surprised, Watson turned to him. "What did you do with the others?"

Horne nodded at the waves gently lapping the remains of the French frigate wrecked on the reef. "Many casualties were scattered along the shoreline, sir. Arms. Legs. Bodies dismembered in the wreck. We dug one common grave for them, sir."

Watson fanned himself faster. "Hmmm. I see."

"At the common grave, sir, we read prayers for Hindus, Muslims, Christians, Buddhists."

"You've been considerate, Horne." Watson squinted in the sun. "In the midst of loss and suffering."

Horne remembered his Marines in attendance close by at the graveside. "We've all suffered, sir."

Watson decided to brighten the conversation, at least to bring the subject back to business.

"Horne, you still haven't asked me why I arrived on this God-forsaken little island."

"No, sir." The sails of Watson's flagship, the *Ferocious*, had appeared on the horizon at that morning's first dawn.

"Aren't you curious, Horne, why I'm here?"

"I'm curious, sir, as to how you found us."

"I discovered you by thinking exactly like you do, Horne. By putting myself inside your head." He frowned. "No easy task. No easy task at all."

Horne tensed. Was Watson going to become one more man trying to understand him, looking for hidden secrets, acting as if he were a puzzle to be deciphered?

Watson continued. "When I decided to come and find you, I studied my maps and suspected that, after leaving Diego-Suarez, you would have sailed down the Madagascar Channel looking for the French treasure ship. When you found nothing—and I had no report that you *had*— a man like you would head northeast. Towards Mauritius. That's what I decided. The nearness of the French headquarters there would not have troubled a man like you. Oh, no."

Horne listened, relieved that Watson was not trying to pry into his innermost thoughts. He was even amused by Watson's smug report of his deduction. He also noted that the Marine Commander-in-Chief had not told him the reason why he had decided to set out in search of him.

The grin on Horne's thin lips irritated Watson. "Damn it, Horne," he ranted, "when a man jeopardises his position, risks the security of his retirement, the last thing in the world he wants is to see someone laughing at him."

The outburst surprised Horne. "I'm sorry, sir. I would never laugh at you, sir."

What had Watson meant by "jeopardising his position" and "risk the security of his retirement"? Horne's curiosity was piqued.

Watson had divulged too much. He knew it, but he still wanted Horne to be, if not grateful, then at least a little more surprised by his sudden arrival.

He pressed, "What would you have done, Horne, had I not appeared?"

The question was naïve and surprised Horne. "Returned to Bombay Castle, sir. Reported to you and submitted my report to Governor Spencer—as it was Spencer who issued my orders."

Watson's bushy eyebrows furrowed. "No, no. Horne. I doubt if Spencer will want a written report on this mission when you return to Bombay Castle. Not with the trouble he's taken to keep the assignment so secret. I suspect he'll follow the pattern the Governors required after your victory at Madras—sealed lips."

Horne reminded Watson, "Sir, we claimed no prisoners-of-war at Madras." He gestured to the three ships in the cove, the *Huma*, the *Tigre* and the recently seized *Calliope*. "But since leaving Madagascar, sir, we've captured fifty-two men. Fifty-three including Captain Le Clerc."

"Le Clerc?" Watson was pleased to change the subject from Governor Spencer. Not knowing what Spencer had said on learning that he had gone to help Horne in the search for the war chest, Watson feared the consequences.

He asked, "What's Le Clerc like, Horne?"

"Arrogant. Angry that he's been posted out here to India. Humiliated at being captured by men he considers to be pirates."

"He has no idea you're connected to the Company?"

"None, sir. I should imagine he'd prefer being taken prisoner by Admiral Pocock and the Royal Navy."

Watson's blue eyes twinkled. "Am I correct, Horne, in believing you don't approve of the man?"

Horne grimaced. "Captain Le Clerc abandoned his crew and an officer aboard the *Tigre*, sir. He left them to defend themselves miserably in a storm while he sailed off safely aboard the *Calliope*."

"Abandoned an officer, Horne?" Watson was surprised. "You didn't tell me you'd captured an officer apart from Le Clerc. Where is he?"

There were many facts Horne had not reported to Watson in the few hours since his arrival. He had chosen to proceed with the work of burying the dead to prevent the bodies from decaying quickly in the heat. He had trusted there would be ample time for a report and discussion.

He answered, "The young officer's name was Gallet, sir. He took his own life. Shortly after we seized the *Calliope*."

"I see." Watson wiped his jowls. "So tell me what you've got out of Le Clerc? Has he talked yet about that bloody war chest?"

"Captain Le Clerc refuses to admit that he came to Oporto to pass on the war chest to another French ship. Yet he does not deny the pattern I suggested to him, the way in which I suspect the cargo's been brought from France, passed from ship to ship."

Watson had already heard Horne's theory about how the French treasure had been passed like a handkerchief or coin at a children's party. He remained more interested in the chest itself.

"But you have seen the war chest, Horne?" he asked anxiously. "You know it's here? On Le Clerc's brig you captured?"

"Yes, I've seen it, sir. But as I explained earlier, I still haven't examined it."

"So what are we waiting for?" Watson settled the cocked hat on his large head. "Let's go out to the *Calliope* and have a look."

Horne was hesitant. "Sir, there's one question I would like to put to you."

"Speak, Horne." Watson was anxious to repair to the French brig.

"What will happen to the *Huma*, sir?"

Watson stared dumbly at him.

"The *Huma*," repeated Horne. "The captured frigate I've been sailing."

Watson's eyes bulged. "I know what the *Huma* is. But do you mean to stand there asking me about a bloody pirate ship when all our futures are at stake?"

This was Watson's second allusion to the uncertainty of their future, Horne noted. What had occurred at Bombay Castle to make the old walrus so uneasy?

Watson rasped, "How do I know what's going to happen in the future when damned Spencer hasn't even fully informed me about this mission?"

"Yes, sir." Horne could not bring himself to apologise for inquiring about the future of the pirate ship. Securing his men's future was more valuable, he felt, than gold in a French war chest. The *Huma* would be a fine vessel for his Marines. A true buccaneer ship.

Watson capitulated slightly; patting Horne's shoulder, he assured him, "Oh, have heart, Horne. Have heart. Given the chance, I'll put a word in Spencer's ear to allow you to keep the *Huma*—that is, if the old crow is still talking to me when we sail into Bombay."

A third reference to trouble between the two men. Horne, however, still refrained from pressing for details.

Instead, he suggested, "The Company could very well rule the *Huma* as a prize for the Maritime Service, sir. A young merchant officer aboard the *Unity* captured the frigate along with a pattimar."

Watson wagged his head. "Yes, yes. Spencer told me about the green Company officer. He also told me how you gave assistance beyond the call of duty."

Blustering, he exclaimed, "Dash it, Horne. Let's stop babbling here in this heat. Let's get out to the *Calliope* and see what's in that bloody chest. That's the only way we'll know if any of us has a future."

"Yes, sir." Horne centred his hat on his forehead.

Watson preceded Horne down the incline, sword clanking against his leg. He waved at the five waiting Marines as he rattled past them, calling, "Come on, lads, let's see if you've done your job, eh?"

The Commander-in-Chief continued down the slope to the open boat bobbing in the surf.

Horne followed Watson, his eyes on the three captured vessels in the cove, the seamen busily working on repairs.

Moving his gaze to the flagship, *Ferocious*, he thought again of Watson's nervous allusions to Governor Spencer. The old walrus was definitely troubled by something.

Babcock nodded to Horne, signalling that he would soon follow him and Watson to the waiting boat. But, first, he and the other Marines wanted to pay their own respects to their dead comrade.

Stepping in front of the grave, Babcock rested his weight on one foot. "You didn't talk much, you ugly Turk, but I'm going to miss you anyway."

Appraising the knotted rope he had taken from Mustafa's corpse on the *Tigre*, he continued, "I don't know where you go from here, Ugly. But wherever it is . . ."

He tossed the garrotte onto the grave. "Here, you might be needing this."

Jingee and Kiro remained standing side by side as Babcock slouched past them down the hill.

After remembering a Hindu prayer for a deceased warrior, Jingee's mind moved from Mustafa to the men he had killed on Oporto. Horne had praised him for accomplishing the land manoeuvre but had cautioned him about becoming too quick to kill, too eager to use his knife when there might be less deadly ways to silence the enemy.

Had he killed too quickly? Could he have spared the Frenchmen's lives instead of slitting their throats? Jingee's pride suffered from Horne's criticism, but he stood stoically by Mustafa's grave and questioned his past actions. He was ready to mend his ways. The main concern in his life was always to please the Captain sahib.

Beside Jingee, Kiro mused over how little Mustafa had spoken to other men. But, then, neither did he himself ever have much to say.

Had Mustafa been trying, too, to achieve some goal he had long ago set for himself? If so, had he achieved it? Kiro thought about the goal of becoming a skilled warrior he had long ago set for himself in Japan. He added a prayer for himself as well as Mustafa. Before Kiro turned away from the grave, he added a third word for Adam Horne, for giving men a chance to live out their dreams.

Jud threw back his head, eyes open, looking at the clouds streaking across the late morning sky. Up there, hidden somewhere in that blue glass bowl, were his wife, his son and, now, Mustafa.

Jud smiled. When would he also go to live in the sky? Jud believed that death was immortality.

Groot set the blue cap on his sun-bleached hair after racking his brain for a prayer for Mustafa. Hurrying down the rocky slope to catch up with Babcock, he called, "Wait, Babcock. I want to apologise."

Babcock did not slow down. "Apologise for what?"

Groot ran. "For laughing at you. For calling you a land lubber yesterday."

"Nothing a cheesehead says could ever bother me, Groot."

"But I want to congratulate you, Babcock. You had a good idea in tricking the enemy onto the reef. Your idea saved us."

"You were at the wheel," Babcock reminded him.

"But it was your idea. It was a very good idea."

Babcock slowed down; he looked at the promontory where the remains of the French frigate were lapped by the Indian Ocean. "My idea doesn't seem so good when you think about how many men it killed."

Groot looked at Babcock. "Are you getting soft?"

Babcock did not answer the question. Instead, he pulled his big ear, asking, "Do you remember how many of us prisoners Horne first took from Bombay Castle to turn into Marines?"

Groot considered. "Ten. Twelve."

"Sixteen. And how many men left Bull Island after training?"

Groot thought. "Seven."

Babcock nodded. "Right. But how many are left now?"

Lowering his eyes to the ground, Groot said, "With Mustafa gone there are only . . . five of us."

"Which one of us is going to be next?" Babcock studied Groot. "Is it going to be you, cheesehead?"

Turning, Babcock continued down the hill to join Horne and Commodore Watson.

Groot did not know if the big American colonial was joking with him or not. He suspected Babcock had been serious, that he was not as carefree as he often pretended.

Groot ran down the hill after him, calling, "What are you going to do with your monkey, Babcock?"

"You ask too many questions, Groot." Babcock waved his hand and kept walking down to the waiting boat.

Aboard the *Calliope*, Horne stood with Commodore Watson and four Marines in the captain's cabin as Jingee hurried in from the companionway, carrying a mallet, a chisel and an iron bar.

Horne took the tools and passed them to the Marine standing next to him, Jud.

Horne, Watson and the Marines crowded around as Jud knelt in front of the iron-banded chest. They watched anxiously as the big African began hitting the mallet against the chisel's wooden butt.

The padlock broke with a snap.

Horne handed Jud the iron bar.

The muscles rose under Jud's ebony-skinned arm as he prised, finally breaking the iron band with his force on the bar.

Rising, he stood back to allow Horne to open the chest's lid.

Horne deferred to Commodore Watson.

Dabbing the handkerchief at his forehead, Watson stepped in front of the bow-topped trunk. Taking a deep breath, he glanced apprehensively at Horne. Then, shaking his head, he hesitated and stood back from the trunk. "No, Horne. It's your victory. You open the lid."

"Victory, sir?" Horne appraised the large chest. "If there's no gold inside, sir, nobody can claim a victory."

"Ah! But if there *is* gold inside, Horne, we'll be welcomed back at Bombay Castle with open arms." Watson looked at the other five Marines. "Who knows? Governor Spencer might be so pleased with your success that he will assign the *Huma* to Horne. She'll be your ship."

Horne and the men exchanged hopeful glances.

Watson added, "And I'll get my pension."

Displeased with himself for mentioning his own worries, he scowled, rasping, "But here you go jabbering again, Horne. Dash it. Open the lid, let's see what's inside."

Watson and the five Marines pushed around Horne. The

hinges creaked as Horne lifted the lid and, then, everybody began to laugh. There was more gold than any of them had ever seen.

END

Adam Horne and the Bombay Marines Adventures

continue in

CHINA FLYER

GLOSSARY

Bilboes—shipboard shackles devised in the Spanish foundries of Bilbao

Brahmin—the highest Hindu caste

Compagnie des Indes Orientales—The French East India Company

Dhoolie—a covered litter

Dhoti—loincloth

Dongi—small canoe made from plantain leaves

Dubash—literally "two languages," hence an interpreter or secretary

Dungri—blue Indian cotton cloth

Howdah—saddle or house on back of elephant

Feringhi—foreigner

Karma—fate or destiny, a person's activities in many reincarnations. Hinduism. Buddhism

Kshatriya—the second highest and Hindu warrior caste

Moong dal—a split pea, frequently used in a savoury pancake batter

Pankration—ancient manner of Greek combat, forerunner of Japanese Karate

Panchama—literally, "the fifth," people outside the four Indian castes

Punkah—overhead fan operated by rope

Sari—female garb, long cloth

Sepoy—Indian troop trained by European standards

Sudra—people below the Hindu high castes

Topiwallah—literally, men with hats; hence, foreigners

Vaisya—the third Hindu caste, the powerful merchant class